TORRID AND

Twisted Tales

OF YOUTH

BY
JOHN RICHARD SPENCER

Table of Contents

<u>Eet And The Apple</u>

In the late 1970s, I found myself traveling on a 3rd-class train trip from Hat Yai to Bangkok, Thailand. After an hour's wait in Hat Yai's crowded but sleepy station, I boarded a rickety wooden carriage belonging to the Royal Siamese Railways. The locomotive bore the stamp '1923' as its year of manufacture. A heavy military presence pervaded the train as a protective measure against Communist guerillas who, at that time, occasionally blew up rolling stock. However, I paid them no mind and sat down with a bottle of Mekong whisky and Coke to guard against the steamy, tropical heat.

Casting my eye along the carriage past the dozens of farmers, students, and the odd soldier, I focused on a stunningly attractive girl facing me from the far end of the carriage. In fact, she was the only object of real interest in sight. She had a striking, determined face, full oval eyes, and black hair shaped in a typically Asian fashion and amongst the shiniest I had ever seen. Her shirt and faded jeans revealed a shapely figure with full, proud breasts. Her lips were full and sensuous and parted into a magnetic smile as her eyes met my gaze. As she smiled, she held up an apple, a decidedly un-tropical fruit. The girl looked to be about nineteen or twenty years old. Her companion was a woman in her early thirties.

At the time, I was a school teacher of twenty-six on holiday. Not being fond of apples, I found myself shaking my head. Not being stupid, however, I instantly changed my mind and seat and bit into the offering. Neither the girl nor her friend could speak a word of English, so the conversation consisted of smiles and the exchange of names. Hers was Eet, and everything about her was delicious. The full, rounded thighs, shapely buttocks, delicate waist, and firm, firm breasts seemed almost to speak to me. I barely noticed her companion's existence. Our visual conversation, interspersed with occasional sign language, was progressing very favorably when suddenly both women stood up and prepared to leave the train in a small town in the middle of nowhere. I couldn't allow those unspoken words to be wasted, so I also alighted and joined them, walking down the main street amidst blank, almost hostile stares from the townspeople.

They led me to a small, dingy, sparsely furnished hotel room. After some Mekong and laughter, the older woman went out for a while. Alone with Eet, I couldn't contain my desire any longer. As she lay on the bed, I slowly loosened each button and removed her shirt and bra, savoring each moment. Her skin was a dusky gold and smelt of musk. Her nipples were hard and erect. As I gingerly ran my tongue down from her eager mouth, I caressed them with the lightest of touches. Her unbuckled jeans revealed an even more perfect body than I had hoped. Those golden thighs and the shaped V mound of her white lace panties were more than I could bear. Hungrily, I flung the jeans to the floor, removing my own dusty apparel almost in the same motion. My rock-like shaft seemed to be playing divining rod as it struggled against the white cotton of her briefs. As I slid this obstacle down, an almost perfect triangle of fine, black pubic hair stared up. Her pussy was already glistening with uncontrolled excitement. The mound of hair and the pink outer lips were just showing; all were soft and inviting. My tongue sang its song, licking inside and out from the inner lips and her wet, hard clitoris to the walls of her vagina themselves. Eet's whole body was shuddering, and her moaning was too definite to be called soft. I clasped her shapely ass and sipped as much of her love juices as I could.

I was rather surprised that, in turn, she didn't go down on me, but apparently, fellatio is generally a 'no no' for Buddhist Thai girls. Climbing on top of Eet's shining wet body, I slowly but determinedly entered her. My shaft pushed into its full length, my hands firmly grasping the rounded cheeks of her behind. Although soaking with juices, her love canal was very, very tight, and my strange journey was being rewarded beyond all anticipation. Up and down, in and out, my pulsating rod plundered that comely flesh, building up to a veritable crescendo. As the index finger of my right hand ever so gently tickled the rim of her anus, my human cucumber thrust faster and faster. It was beyond all control. The proud breasts, the firm, shapely ass, and the fine, black fur tickling my shaft as it made its way obscured everything else; the place, the time, and even the identity itself. As my inevitable explosion occurred, the screams of her orgasms filled the air.

As we lay there still naked and steaming, the older woman re-entered the room. She looked, smiled, and, pointing at Eet, pronounced the word 'dek.' I had no idea what she meant, so I ignored it. She then removed her clothing and began dancing around the room naked. She didn't particularly turn me on, so I made no moves in that regard. Again, I made sexually tropical love with Eet, and the other woman seemed to get a kick out of standing there in the nude watching us. The lovemaking was so intense that after this round, Eet's moist, beckoning vagina and my own missile could take no more. Beyond pleasure, there was pain.

Both ladies saw me back to the little railway station in the middle of nowhere to catch the next once-a-day train. The one in her thirties kept pointing to the younger one and repeating 'dek.' The penny finally dropped. 'Dek' is the Thai word for a baby. She was Eet's mother.

The End

(C) 1991 John Spencer

A Shot In Hospital

I had just finished a shower and a fast but intense round of the old in and out with my defacto. There is something about the tropical heat. The hotter it gets, the hotter you get. With her fanny juice still on the old fella, I had to get dressed to go out.

I had this appointment with this really horny 22 yr old chick who had great legs, succulent tits, and a curvaceous arse to boot. Vicky, with her sleek shoulder length, black hair, and cute face, had begged me to take her for a ride on my 360cc motorcycle and I had a feeling I was going to get lucky.

She was waiting for me when the bike screeched to a halt. Her tight blue jeans seemed to get tighter every second, and the bar that had sprung up between my legs made an uncomfortable contact with the gas tank. On she climbed and as we sped off to play with the traffic in the afternoon sun, I could feel the quivering vibrations of her thighs. They have this quaint habit of driving on the right or in the middle, in the Philippines, as the mood strikes them but I managed to get it right. We rode just over the bridge to Mactan, round and round, and back to Cebu.

A bit of wining and dining, and it was time to turn the lady's thoughts to love. My thoughts had been there all the time. Transforming romance and true love into a quick fuck at a motel is no easy task, but somehow, I managed to get this chick's agreement.

Into the dark, we zoomed, heading towards Queensland Lodge (the only connection with our illustrious state in Oz is the name, palm trees, and bananas).

My cock was pointing the way, that is until we reached the large cement block, smack bang in the middle of Manilili Street. There we were, lying in a sprawled heap under the bike. My right leg was bleeding (20 stitches worth), and Vicky had a swollen wrist. The jeepney, which had nearly run us over, took us to the hospital (for a fee), and we were both admitted to a small private room without even a fan.

There we lay, Vicky on her bed and me on mine with my leg in a thousand bandages. Damned if I was going to miss out on my fuck, injured or not. I called her over since she could still walk and asked her to undress and comfort me. She had stopped crying by this time and obliged. I pulled her knickers off within 15 seconds of her climbing onto my bed. Her triangle of cute pubic hairs surrounded a juicy love niche. I could just turn enough to push my still rock-hard shaft deep into that beckoning cavity. Vicky provided the necessary movement, pumping me for all she was worth, and after I had shot my load, even my leg felt better.

My defacto walked in the next morning, took one look, and walked out. Vicky and her sprained wrist were discharged an hour later. At that moment, twenty student nurses gathered around my bed. Things were looking up.

The End

© 1994 John Spencer

The Last Fuhrer

From the podium, Condrad Radske screamed hate against the evils befalling the land. "What once was a simple, pure country is now a sinister polyglot with hidden motives and distrust everywhere. It is almost impossible to find the enemy, let alone destroy him. But, friends, I have located that enemy, that evil in our midst!"

Conrad Ratske was actually born and christened "Paul Smith," but he had long ago changed his name for a more Teutonic one. Deutschland had fathered Hegel and his doctrine of world Spirit and national consciousness; it had given birth to Frederick Nietzsche and his theory of the Superman who was Nature's king. The Fatherland had also been home to the great Adolf Hitler, whose fight for a clean world had been defeated by the same insidious, polyglot enemy as faced this country now. True, Germany had also produced Karl Marx, but then again, he was a Jew, and Conrad (Paul) chose to overlook that incidental fact.

Conrad had drawn together considerable elements of the population who were dissatisfied with the nation and their own personal progress. The dispossessed, the friendless, the lonely, the persecuted, and all other elements of society's leftovers that he could find: the white ones, that is. His following became larger and larger, and eventually, the country's security forces were forced to take little notice of him even though they considered such attention beneath their dignity. Conrad had, however, been a devoted student of Mein Kampf and knew all about the "martyr effect." The more the authorities tried to close down his message, the larger his following became.

"People of the true land," he raged, "that enemy is all around us. It is the destruction of race consciousness and the combining of things that were never meant to be combined." His brown uniform was soaked in sweat, and even the swastika substitute on his left arm looked a tad tawdry. "Coloreds from all over the earth have swamped us. Inferior cultures demand their 'right' to supplant ours. Women are told they should be men, and at this very moment, as I am speaking, the Jews are engineering the final destruction of Palestine. Dogs and cats keep a respectable distance from each other, let alone mate. Why should our great nation be reduced to a mess of square triangles?"

Thwap! A rotten tomato landed square on his chin. While the crowd was soundly beating the alleged thrower, he wiped the unasked-for source of vitamin C from his face and continued. "We are never safe from unnatural evil. This attempted assassination is more than sufficient proof of what I'm saying." His voice had reached a crescendo. "Even our own dearly loved native folk are getting strange ideas which will destroy both them and us. We must act now! Before it is too late!"

At that moment, a young blonde girl stepped up next to Conrad and slowly, tantalizingly began to remove her shirt. Her proud, erect bosoms with their pink nipples gazed brazenly at the crowd. The tiny red marks on them, allegedly from police beatings, were too faint to be seen at any distance. "Please, Sharna, go on." Conrad's voice softened for the first time that evening. Trying to look coy and embarrassed, the girl unhitched her belt and dropped her brown trousers. The panties quickly followed, and she just stood there, her richly endowed pubic mound the focus of much of the audience's gaze. "Now, Sharna, please turn around." Conrad attempted to sound like a doctor but didn't make it.

Her back to the crowd and the succulent rounded cheeks of her backside in full view, the audience was asked to focus on a purple mark in the shape of a butterfly. (It could have been a failed tattoo or an accidental bruise; it could have been anything.) "People of the nation," Conrad's voice echoed. "This hideous scar was inflicted on this innocent girl by a group of foreigners who claimed she insulted them! Isn't this an awful, disgusting sight?" The women present screamed in agreement, and the men did their best to complain about what they were being forced to witness. Conrad went on and on. "I am what I am today because of my pure bloodlines. I'm proud to be a pedigree human. I'm so proud of it that I have hired an independent firm of genealogists to trace my entire family tree back 500 years. It's all in the blood, you know. At the next unified rally of our National Salvation Party, the results of that search will be handed to me in a sealed envelope, and I will publicly announce them. My wife's family and their racial pride will also be researched and demonstrated."

The crowd roared approval and screamed, "Hail Conrad. Long live our homeland," in unison and a pathetic attempt at German accents. Demonstrations, rallies, and street marches were everywhere. Incidents of racially motivated violence were dramatically on the increase, and the government was extremely worried.

"Why doesn't Conrad simply have an accident?" suggested the minister in charge of public happiness. The fact that this minister was an ex-policeman didn't help convince his colleagues of all of his novel ideas. "No, no, no!" intoned the Prime Minister. "The mobs are mobilized already. Make a martyr of our Paul, I mean Conrad, and they'll just find another idiot to lead them."

The leaders of the government had no bright ideas. The situation was getting totally out of hand. Seventeen immigrants had been brutally murdered in the last week alone. There was no constitutional way of preventing Conrad and his party from standing at the next election, which was only a year away, and their prospects looked alarmingly good. The only thing the ministers could agree on was moving their very "modest" personal wealth and assets offshore and meeting in Bermuda if the worst came to the worst.

It was a sunny October afternoon. 150,000 people had assembled for the national rally, eagerly waiting for Paul's (I mean Conrad's) message of hate. "White is clean; anything else is not quite so clean," Conrad ranted to the crowd. "If color was better than white, why do you use bleach on your clothes, and why isn't dirt white? No, friends. Color, where it doesn't belong, must be swept away. And I, as the Fuhrer of our country, am just the broom or mop to do it."

A fat lady with huge knockers climbed up next to Conrad and whispered in his ear. He paused, then addressed the multitude again. "It is time!" he yelled. "Time to show you, the true people, what my family and I are really made of. Nietzsche's Superman stands before you, proud that he is the best. I have my entire family history in my hands." The fat lady whispered again and tried to snatch back the envelope. Conrad would have none of it.

He tore open this obstruction to the final truth, yeah, the final solution to the world's problems, and read from the page before him." Elsa Radske, maiden name Elsa Jones: daughter of Jacob Jones and Reissa Lad. Granddaughter of ..... and great-granddaughter of Ahahib Sratnanee, an immigrant from Pakistan. Conrad Radske: the son of Richard Smith and Ruthe Rubenstein, the latter being a survivor of Auschwitz."

The paper fell from his hand. The beautiful Sharna, who was also his mistress as well as his stooge, spat on him and farted in his face. Conrad turned purple and tried to run but slipped on a banana peel and fell off the podium. He landed headfirst and broke his neck. The crowd booed and simply went home, but not before a loudmouth yelled, "Go on, Sharna. Show us your injuries again."

The End

(c) 1994 John Spencer

The Librarian

It is late afternoon, about 30 minutes before closing time, when I enter the library to do some research. The modest little brick building is almost deserted, with just one elderly lady reading at a table and a schoolboy at the photocopier. The silence is almost unbearable.

I need some help with my book list, so I look for a staff member, but no one is there. Then, behind a book stack, I see her. The librarian is a stunning girl of about thirty with horn-rimmed glasses, emphasizing her intelligence but failing to suppress her oozing sexuality. Standing on a step stool, she is trying to shelve some books but can't quite reach them. In the effort, her short blue skirt rides up, revealing a triangle of white cotton and more than a hint of sumptuous and curvaceous backside. The harder she tries, the more tantalizing the oscillation of her thighs becomes.

After perusing her seat of learning for a couple of minutes, I cough to attract her attention. She spins round, drops all the books, and, losing her balance, falls straight into my arms, uttering a small "Oooh" full of promise. Her top shelf is well and truly stacked and begging for display as her nipples stiffen under a floral blouse.

"I'm studying Kant," I mumble as she regains her balance. "You can't what?" she purrs as her blue eyes scan my manhood through the horn-rimmed glasses. Before I can reply, she strides over to the entrance and, observing that the library is now empty, locks the door. With a professorial air of confidence, she asserts, "The library is now closed, but I'm not." Unfastening her skirt, she discards it and pulls down her panties of white cotton. Her sandy-colored and forested delta beckons to this explorer. Still wearing her glasses, she pushes me onto the Loans desk, snatching my trousers and jocks as if they were overdue loans.

As she bends down, her tongue seeks congress with my pointer to make sure that it is paying full attention. The silken lips glide up and down with a studied motion, leaving a trace of red lipstick on my straining joystick. At that moment, she stands back, admiring the results of her preliminary research. Then she discards her blouse and is naked save for her spectacles.

Ever so slowly, she lowers herself onto me, the moist lips of her Special Reserve section engulfing my now throbbing cock. The penetration is deep and totally mind-blowing. Her love tunnel is flooded with raging juices. I can see the soft cheeks of her silky arse vibrating as she picks up speed. We both explode together in a violent convulsion that sends body fluids dribbling onto the desk and across some newly returned magazines.

"That is all you'll ever need to know about the subject of Cunt," she says with an intellectual smile, and I leave my local library feeling a total satisfaction and a joy of knowledge.

The End

(C) 1995 John Spencer

<u>Devil Boy</u>

He was a really nice guy. It wasn't his fault that he had been thrown out of the church choir and that he wasn't good enough for the school football team. Jason was a pure spirit. He met kindness with kindness and tried his best when he met the other. He was never quite good enough to make any of the teams, but he gave his best. Who could ask for more than that?

Jason grew up and went to university and all but couldn't quite make it. By the time he graduated as a mining engineer, the recession was well and truly underway. His first employment was with a prominent mining company in the Northern Territory. Jason was not a racist by any means. The aboriginal folk in the locality quickly became his friends. He could understand their misery, caught between cultures and methods. He could understand their lack of hope in tomorrow and their fondness for booze. Although he was white, he didn't belong either. It was a pure stroke of luck that he'd got a job at all on graduation.

Jason carried on with his wholeness of spirit. It's in the genes, after all. Those with a loving nature will always treat the world as their friend. As for the other kind, we know where to find them. This lad was the kind of human being we all love to cherish. Not only a true-blue Aussie but also a true-blue human being. He had no enemies at all, that is, until the day of the death of the elder.

It was not the fault of the rainbow serpent that the elder had died. The old folk said that Jinjarrabee had once killed a snake, for no good reason, in his youth, and that's why his death came early. The younger members of the tribe attributed his demise to a fondness for cheap plonk, but then again, youths are so cynical. How could a white man ever hope to resolve such a problem? No chance. However, it was Jason's job to ensure the cooperation of the Aboriginal people with his company. After all, the company offered money and didn't destroy the natural habitat that much. A few sacred sites only; the company was sorry, but so what?

It wasn't just the bosses of the company that said this; the big white bosses in Canberra said the same thing. There would definitely be a place for all Australians, no matter their color or economic condition, in the new democratic, multicultural Australia. The government, with its magic cloud, would instantly make all Australians equal and ensure the coming of the Dreamtime for all, black, white, or brindle.

Sadly, it didn't happen. The great white elders in Canberra had lied again. The empty flagons still littered the settlement, and the flies still showed no letup in their attack on the children. Nobody had been able to convince the elders (or the younger for that matter) that money could replace a lost soul or life. So, the task finally fell to Jason, youthful though he was. He was all the company had left.

He just told them what would happen and that he was sorry. It really wasn't his personal fault. At the moment of his speaking, a dingo came and licked his hand. When Jason spoke, most of the elders listened, but for no reason they could understand. Some other white folks had told them that Jason was a loser and would always be a loser and that the black fellers who sided with him would suffer a similar fate.

The amazing gods in Canberra finally gave land rights to the indigenous tribal folk, that is, to all the other tribes. Just because their tribe was sitting in the middle of a mining "boom," the courts passed them over. They all loved Jason. Although he was a white man and worked for the company that threatened their existence, he was a kindred spirit. He was a white Aborigine. He was one of the few people who could really understand the difference between the Rainbow Serpent, a flagon of plonk, and a "White Lady."

The time came for a reckoning between the Rainbow Serpent and the great white gods in Canberra. A small man with a poxy face appeared. He had come to speak on behalf of both the mining company and the great white "chiefs" in Canberra. He continued, "Jason, for his own personal gain, had defied the company's intention for further progress and wealth for everybody and was responsible for the tribe missing out on a big financial settlement. "Jason is a devil boy," the man had said. "He has seeds of evil that are older than the Great Rainbow Serpent and the Dreamtime itself.

It was true. Jason came from the old time and knew every one of the nine names of the devil. He was ultimately evil personified and had been described vaguely in one of the books of the Old Testament. It was carefully explained to the tribal folk that this seeming friend was a creature of darkness. An American minister came to the settlement and called on God to strike Jason down. "Evil comes in all forms, my friends," he had said. "See if I'm not right."

This all happened too fast. Lightning broke the sky, and as Jason walked from the small cafe where he had eaten his evening meal, a flash of lightning struck him dead in the middle of the town's main street. The minister of religion came running out from his hotel with the town mayor behind him. "I told you so," he cried, "that man was from the devil, a real 666!" The aboriginal folk present just stared with disbelief.

Just then, an elder who also professed the white man's religion warned the folk that Jason had surely come from the devil. The old folk and the young all agreed Jason was truly a devil man. Into the town square strode a new missionary, secure with the knowledge of the faith and conversion of these heathen folk. He looked the gathering in the square in the eye and told them that Jason was a harbinger of evil, both in terms of the Christian religion and in terms of the Dreamtime.

A very old man gazed up at him. "I know the messengers of hell when I see them." The missionary smiled. He continued with the arrogance of faith, "Jason was truly evil, an enemy of the Rainbow Serpent, and has been described in our old books as Beelzebub. All religions are the same. Jason is our final enemy."

The aboriginal folk continued to stare with mouths slightly open.

Everyone agreed that Jason was the personification of evil in any language or symbolism. Then, the missionary spoke with that final authority that can only be earned. "Jason was cruel, vicious, and self-seeking, I believe. He led you people astray from the truth and progress."

A young girl, maybe twelve years old, lifted her eyes to the stranger and screamed, "I know Jason was evil, but he was kind! He didn't even kill snakes!"

The End

(c) 1994 John Spencer

Edna and the Asis Man

Edna was just seventeen years old with a face like an angel and a body that would surely attract those from other places. She had grown up in the northern province of Cebu. Her high school sweetheart had ruined her reputation and then promptly abandoned her. Therefore, she had to fend for herself at an early age. As a waitress/hospitality girl, she could just earn a living.

Few foreigners entered the establishment where she worked, as it specialized in serving warm beer at high prices. Plenty of Japanese came, though, with their customary grunting and pinching, any chance they got. That was about all until the night of the cloak and dagger. Gunfire had echoed outside sporadically for thirty minutes. The customers had remarked on the law-and-order problem but continued drinking.

Into the bar staggered a tall blond man, his left arm covered in blood. "Give me an ice-cold one, and quick," he yelled. The beer soon materialized, as did the shapely young Edna. "You're hurt," she crooned sympathetically. "All in a night's work," came the casual reply from the stranger. Sirens wailed in the distance. "Criminal ka?" inquired the sexy seventeen-year-old. "No," wheezed the wounded Roger. "I'm a kind of international policeman," and left it at that. The girl dutifully brought hot /towels and iodine and bathed his wound. It wasn't too serious, just a graze. The cold beer in one hand and the warm girl in the other soon revived the stranger's spirits. The feel of shapely flesh pressed close against his own was a definite improvement on the inherent danger of the streets.

Of course, for every thousand innocent tourists who are accused of being CIA plants or international criminals by passing drunks, there is always one person who passes unnoticed and really does have something to hide. And so it was with Roger. His main weapon was his mouth. His task was to encourage a right-wing military coup (successful) against the government. A bit of money here, a payoff there, and things proceeded swimmingly. The only reason he had had the brief fling with a passing bullet was that he had been mistaken for a fleeing hold-up man in the dark by an off-duty policeman. His real crimes remained totally undetected and unsuspected. Roger's social habits, both cold and warm, in addition to a delicate assignment, made the normal diplomatic cover impossible. The Asis man was forced to pass, convincingly, I might add, as a debauched tourist.

Edna had a smattering of class about her despite her occupation, and she studiously avoided associations with customers outside of working hours. Yet, there was something special about this blond stranger. During the ensuing week or so, he returned several times. If it wasn't love, it was a damned good substitute. The following few days saw a flowering passion of the hot and sticky kind emerge between the lovely Edna and the devious Roger.

Although she didn't yet know it, Edna was very pregnant. Fortunately for her, Roger was also smitten with the love bug. He married her and applied for her visa with the embassy. Considering his connections, it would undoubtedly come through in a couple of weeks.

Meanwhile, he dutifully went about his assignment. Within three months, he could count on an armed insurrection involving an initial contingent of nearly an entire division. His superiors would be thrilled, and he could surely count on a promotion. Most third-world governments have lots of natural enemies waiting in the wings for any semblance of a chance. Roger's job requires establishing the groundwork without being detected. At this, he was indeed a master. His entire assignment had been completed, and nobody was any the wiser. All he had to do now was wait for Edna's visa, and then he could return home to a hero's welcome with his bride.

The visa formalities were almost complete. Any day now, the visa would be granted. The Asis man left the Philippines first and provided his wife with the necessary money and accouterments to follow him a few days later. A job well done and a rosy future beckoned.

Not one day after his departure from the country, the proverbial brown stuff hit the fan. Whole battalions of soldiers were confined to barracks. Armed police and military men of all descriptions combed the country, looking for Roger. They couldn't find him, but his lovely bride was quickly arrested. She was obviously a prime suspect in the whole messy business. The "routine" questioning of the lass gave her a new perspective on the meaning of "sex," caused her to have a miscarriage, and brought about her untimely death a few days later.

The Asis nan, unaware of the fate of his bride, was on his way to work in lovely, suburban Melbourne when a .22 caliber bullet made a neat little hole in the back of his head.

In a plush office in the senior regional embassy, two rather senior diplomats were having a morning brandy. "We've been trying to get rid of that bastard for years. He finally made it easy for us." The wheels of government ground on Illegal immigrants by the thousand enjoyed the Australian climate, genuine would-be immigrants were given the run-around, and it was business as usual. The cocktail parties raged in the outposts abroad, and the diplomats smiled at one another.

"He was never one of us, you know, " remarked a middle-ranking diplomat when questioned about Roger's accident during a Christmas party. "He probably had links to the mob."

The End

© **1995 John Spencer**

A Message from God

Mark Rost had never been a stunner; it wasn't him that the girls' basketball teams turned around to look at during breaks in the game. On those rare occasions when his hopes rose, he invariably spotted the usual, rugged guy just behind him in their line of sight. However, Mark was more than an expert wanker, His nightly fantasies were like an internal thunderstorm, and none of his friends ever asked to borrow his magazines.

You can imagine his interest when he first heard the news; the sperm bank program was looking for donors and would pay hard, cold cash for the same stuff Mark gave away for free, nightly. Artificial insemination had answered the prayers of thousands of childless couples, but the injectables had, of course, to be obtained from somewhere.

Vanity can get the better of most of us. If he didn't get the chance to perform the deed, at least his seed would be sown while he earned some beer money. Besides, genetically (apart from his looks), he was more than O.K. He rated in the top ten percent in all IQ tests. His ancestors had dutifully participated in all the country's wars. None of his relatives had ever been in prison. Mark was, indeed, the ideal sperm bank material. Besides that, he was available; he had no steady job or other problematic occupier of time and could perform at short notice (at the proverbial drop of a pin, so to speak) or at the sight of a cute nurse in her uniform,

It was agreed by the doctors in charge of the program less than ten minutes after Mark had departed. He was indeed just what they were so short of. Thirty percent of the entire program could be met by this one single man alone. In a nation of wankers, it is really hard to find a suitable one when you need one; and so it came about that Mark would make twice weekly visits to the hospital and was always treated with much more respect than he was generally accustomed to. The sexy nurses smiled harder than normal, wiggling their assets as he passed by. They tried their best to ignore his lack of sexual presence, his pimpled, pock-marked face, and his general demeanor. Mr. Wrong, the medical staff, and the administrators greeted him with more than mere deference; yeah, perhaps a sense of importance. Mark felt like the doctors' edition of John Holmes. After all, true talent will always come out, no matter where it lies hidden,

Once inside the donation area, Mark, who needed little encouragement, was shown films about the Miss Universe pageant and other suitable photographic material. His performance, at first, was faultless. Then, he became seasoned. The opportunities were just a little greater than a bit of attention and small money. "I don't know why, Doc, but the pictures aren't doing anything for me, I'm having trouble today,"

It was a touch unprofessional, but Mark's donations to the A.I. program were so successful and such a money spinner for the hospital that a couple of nurses were persuaded to do a strip for the pimpled lad. The results were carried away to the waiting recipients. Wanking, smoking, and drinking are, alas, like blackmail. They start out small but move inexorably toward the big time.

The prime donor had become very difficult. He had gone home several times without leaving his genetic legacy. "But when you're on a winner after years of drought, better give it a go," mused Mark. Much as the world likes to try, it is always hard to equate money and sex and the products thereof. The giving man acquired a hungry look in his eye,

"No way," said Rita, the sexiest blonde nurse in the place, "I won't do it." "But," said the director of the hospital, "It's worth more than your job or mine if you don't. Besides a little touching here and there, exposing yourself at the right moments and the occasional touch of partial fellatio isn't all that bad."

And so it came about that Mark had live, interactive encouragement before he was required to perform his task, The program was so, so successful that the directors regarded the young man as a Godsend. His seed had produced a 95% success rate against the average of 20%. Not only that, but the parents were totally happy with what they got: bouncing baby boys or girls who were both intelligent and had the looks of the gods.

This game of economic, sexual, and genetic cat and mouse had continued for years, and there were veritable squads of young ladies in white uniforms who were obliged to go the whole hog with Mark. The hospital, in fact, had developed its own technique for removing sperm from the relevant vagina and transferring it to a test tube of the right temperature,

Mark's initial genetic children were now more than ten years old. Two of them had killed and mutilated people, another five had been convicted in juvenile court for arson, and thirty-seven had minor criminal records. Mark didn't know why he was told never to return, and seven nurses spat on him on his way out. "How can such a good wicket show tricky spin," he thought, "Never mind, it'll come good again." It didn't come good. As the police led him away, he was confused, "What have I done?" he screamed.

The law moves in mysterious ways, The nation was one of the first to pioneer artificial insemination programs and was one of the first to recognize genetic value and potential. Unfortunately for Mark, it was also one of the first to enact a genetic criminal code and make it retrospective.

"All this modern science," mumbled the executioner as he fastened the rope around Mark's neck. "The good book always told us, 'Take out the mad dog and shoot him. As ye sow, so shall ye reap."

Down the road, not more than a hundred meters away, a child at that moment had just stabbed its mother.

The End

© 1994 John Spencer

High Jinks In The Highlands

The city of Edinburgh in Scotland in late summer is picturesque but in a gray sort of way, making it a place of shadows and soft lights. It is also cold for an Australian who is used to warm climates. I had come up from London by bus in 1974 while on a long working holiday. It became obvious early in the piece that, with my limited finances, I would have to find a young lassie in order to keep warm. To save money and to spur myself on, I seldom took a hotel room. The drab railway stations and the leafy parks became my home. Each evening, I would frequent the local pubs. The music, the beer, and the company were all good, but I'd had no luck in my search for a girl. I had made the acquaintance of several other travelers (male) but was no closer to my goal of warmth and fulfillment.

One evening, towards the end of August, I increased my resolve. In the company of another Australian called Bruce, who was also in his early twenties, I did the usual round of pubs, finishing at Nikky Tam's down the bottom of the Royal Mile. The local girls were polite and friendly but hardly eager.

At closing time (10 pm!), we stepped into the street unaccompanied. Worried but still determined, I trod the remaining cobblestones at the end of the Royal Mile. Ahead were two tall blondes, shapely legs showing beneath their overcoats.

Quickening pace, I caught up to them, my friend following behind, and attempted to engage them in conversation. Slightly to my surprise, my lame words, "Do you girls know any pubs that are still open?" did not meet with instant rejection. There were no places open after ten, but the ladies were interested. After some brief small talk, they paired themselves off and led us to a moonlit botanical garden. Both Jinty and Kim were nurses at a city hospital. Jinty was taller and, to my mind, the prettier of the two, with long blonde hair and crystal-clear blue eyes. She had obviously fancied me from the first moment of our chance encounter. In the park, we sat facing a lake complete with parading ducks. Jinty's lips were full and moist, and her slim, curved body was firm in my embrace. Not being a very forward young man, I was a little tentative. That first kiss on Jinty's red lips was met with a passionate response, her tongue exploring with abandon.

Both girls shared a bed-sitting room where visitors were forbidden at night, especially of the male variety. The chilly night air and her enthusiasm caused Jinty to decide to risk it. Her flatmate concurred, and after a short walk and tip-toe to the entrance, we found ourselves in a large, comfortable, feminine room with green and blue drapes and two large beds. Kim and Bruce climbed into theirs, still dressed, and settled down in what appeared to be fairly innocent embraces. Jinty disappeared into the bathroom, leaving me sitting on her bed, a little uncertain of the situation. She soon returned, wearing the flimsiest provocative nighties, and entered the bed. Removing my shirt and trousers, I did likewise.

Her desire was evident as I kissed her and ran my hands over her rounded breasts, down her smooth waist, and onto her shapely thighs and the delicious curve of her backside. To my surprise, she wasn't wearing anything under the night dress. Her bush of ashen blonde pubic hair tantalized my fingers, and her shapely love box opened to my touch. Her vagina was sweet-smelling, warm, and very wet. Jinty's long, velvety fingers caressed my balls ever so gently and fastened with the litheness of a python around my straining cock. With the caress of a summer breeze, she teased both the head and the shaft. Her delicious aperture seemed to be gaining heat by the second. She pressed her supple body against mine, her juicy pussy with its blonde forest teasing my throbbing rod unbearably.

Mindless of the other couple in the room, she climbed on top of me and guided my eager penis into her tunnel. As the head, then the shaft, went in, I was in ecstasy. The warmth, the wetness, and her pulsating vaginal muscles were mind-blowing. With my hands caressing every inch of her polished ass, Jinty effortlessly ground up and down on my throbbing member. Gone were all vestiges of the gray cold. She was one of the most beautiful girls I had ever seen, let alone got to fuck. Fragrant nectars ran out of her, saturating my entire scrotum. As she increased her speed into a frenzy, my pride of manhood discharged with the ferocity of a cannon. Her earthy perfume filled the air, and my load of jism filled her box. As she climaxed, her thighs began trembling. ·

Sure enough, the next morning, the archetypal puritanical landlady gave both girls their notice, and Bruce set off alone on his travels. Kim, Jinty, and I decided to rent an apartment, but first, Jinty and I agreed to take a short trip to the highlands. The train chugged past some of the more famous lochs, including Loch Lomond, which is the very sight that turns one's thoughts to love. There were no other people in our compartment, so we felt unrestricted. Jinty was wearing a low-cut, clinging black dress, which displayed to great advantage her ample breasts and sensuous thighs. Raising her dress, she placed my hand on her crotch and then inside her briefs. Her furry snatch was as warm, moist, and ready for action as it had been the night before. The compartment door couldn't be locked, but all thoughts of self-restraint were gone. With a tantalizing movement, her delicate fingers unzipped my fly, and her sensual lips, lipstick and all, lovingly closed around my enlarged dick. Each flick of her tongue and expert lip movement sent spasms of joy through every erotic zone of my being. When I finally exploded, she swallowed hard, leaving traces of my glistening cum on her lips. Then she smiled, and her natural sensuality caused me to go hard again almost immediately.

Jinty lifted her dress right up, exposing the badge of her womanhood to the light of day. She begged me to go down on her, and there was no way I was going to deny that delicious body. I savored the musty female scent that emanated from her love hole and set to my joyous task. Her vaginal lips and their enclosed jewel were swollen with sheer animal passion. The taste of her fluids left hot dinners for dead. Although I was previously inexperienced in this aspect of lovemaking, her cries of pleasure impressed me and probably the passengers in the next compartment as well. Dropping my jeans and briefs, I positioned myself over her, with her slender legs on my shoulders, and thrust deep inside her. The heat from our coitus had entirely fogged up the windows and steamed the whole compartment. With all control gone, our mutual thrusting rivaled the engine's pistons in intensity. About twenty seconds after the whistle sounded, almost simultaneous orgasms filled the air with other noises, and Jinty's legs were quivering. Our juices trickled down from her vaginal entrance and dripped onto the carriage seat.

In the months ahead, equally exciting repetitions of that lovemaking were to occur countless times, often with the winter snowflakes falling.

The End

© John Spencer

The Man Who Hated Words

It was 9:45 on the morning of March 5, 1999. Craig Stephens was poring over a pile of papers on his desk in the Sydney office of the Bureau of Statistics. Australia was ruled by the Progressive Wealth Party under the leader- ship of Prime Minister Falcon. The Progressive Wealth Party had established the nation as an icon of international consciousness; a third-world country, yes, but very internationally conscious. Low wages, high prices, and few job opportunities were the order of the day. Despite these less-than-ideal conditions for the lucky country, civil disturbances were few, thanks to the new computer-based police identification and security system. To add insult to injury, English was only featured on street signs in subtitles as a second language.

"Hi, Craig." Sue, the departmental head's secretary, was leaning over him, her long brown hair flickering over his papers. "I wonder if you could help me to spend a free evening on Friday with a successful, handsome man?" "I'd be delighted," stammered Craig. "Great. Please give a message to Alan in Accounts that he is expected at my place for dinner at 8 pm." Craig's face reddened as he found himself mumbling assent. His position as a grade 3 clerk with the bureau could hardly be considered the pinnacle of success. Although he had finished fifth in the State for Mathematics in the 1988 HSC and had graduated from University with an honors Science degree, he had never been able to find a career commensurate with his potential. During interviews, Craig found himself struggling with the answers to even the simplest of questions. It was only as a smaller cog in the bureaucratic wheel that he had managed to find any niche at all in the career world.

Many of society's functions in the Australia of 1999 had been reduced to numbers with the advent of the computerized I.D. system. Work, purchases of goods, and even the expenditure of leisure time and money were all defined and governed according to the allocated numbers.

Within the drabness of the planned environment, Craig was comfortable, if not content. However, humans still had to talk, express feelings and desires, fall in love, and breed.

With all the loss of individuality and personal freedom in a new and uniform world, there was still not only scope for personal expression, there was a need for it.

Although a well-built young man of twenty-five with rather distinctive good looks, Craig had never been popular. All through high school, he had remained without a girlfriend. Despite his Reebok running shoes and Adidas accessories, Craig was not 'cool.' Rarely did he have a date for the school dances, and when he did, the girl would often think he was some sort of jerk and refuse to go out with him again.

The end of the school dance of October 1988 occurred on a balmy Friday evening. Craig had brought Jessica, a moderately attractive slim blonde, as his partner. When she had accepted his invitation, he thought his luck with girls had changed. Jessica was an intellectual type of girl with glasses and good grades, but she had a well-curved figure, and she seemed to like him. After the dance, Craig and Jessica drove to the planned student beach party. The bonfire, the music, and the wine were all agreeable against the background of the rolling surf.

The awkward lad drew the girl to him and kissed her. To his total surprise, she responded with definite enthusiasm. "I like men who take risks," Jessica purred. "I'm a bit of a gambler myself," stated Craig with a greater-than-usual degree of boldness. "I sometimes used to copy the English essays of Fred Stone in the A class, and at the cricket final last season, when I was the last batsman in, I threw caution to the wind and went for the bash." The girl just looked at the sand.

The others left early, and Jessica and Craig found themselves alone in the soft hue of the fire. Their kisses grew stronger, and Jessica pushed close in his embrace. Craig's heart was pounding, and he was consumed with desire. "Be careful," murmured Jessica. "I might get into trouble". "What? You'll be in trouble with your parents for coming home late?" stammered the boy. She didn't answer, merely gazing into the sea. "Take me home, please," she finally replied.

Craig never saw Jessica again. After leaving school, he fared no better with the ladies. With peroxided locks, the young man took the headlong plunge into serious surfing. To the purchase of the latest twin finned board and metallic blue panel van, neither of which he could really afford, Craig added a rigorous dedication. Being an accomplished surfer was necessary but not sufficient.

He looked like, sounded like, and even smelled like the roughest cult member. Down to the unshaven jaw, the unwashed hair, and the dirty, torn jeans, he fitted the image.

The crowd to which Craig attempted to belong included assorted rebellious youths, some with quite heavy drug convictions, school dropouts, and runaway teenage girls. Although none of the female members could have accurately been described as young 'ladies,' a number of them were physically attractive, particularly to Craig.

Cathy was a shapely sixteen-year-old with shoulder-length, dark hair, while Liz was a fourteen-year-old natural blonde. Both girls were wild, fast, and none too discerning with their favors. Like the others, their language reflected youthful impatience and contempt for all authority. Craig repeatedly 'moved' on both Liz and Cathy but to no avail. They were a world away from him.

When he used the four-letter 'in' words with either girl, the response was merely a smirk. Once, he had asked Cathy if she would like to go for a drive in his van. "Forget it, ya dork," snapped the cool, cool, dark-haired girl in her miniscule white bikini. At that moment, Ted, a seasoned 'surf' of about twenty-seven, yelled, " Get ya butt in 'ere! "and Cathy walked over to his wagon, obeying without question.

"Dork." That was the general opinion of Craig held around the surf scene. His natural good manners and general lack of aggression hadn't helped much either. With the advent of the national I.D. and security system, the surfie fraternity had virtually ceased to exist almost overnight. The tighter control of leisure time and money ended more than the surfing scholarships, but Craig had opted out long before. About the time he was accepted into the Bureau of Statistics, he had decided on a complete image reversal.

Gone were the panel van and board. In their place were a luxury car and a habit of drinking Southern Comfort socially. The new Craig was no more affordable than the old. What scope there was for overspending within the system of credits and numbers, Craig achieved with ease. Upon being informed that he would have no annual vacation at the end of his second year as a clerk, the now aspiring yuppie was dumbfounded. The departmental head pointed to Craig's I.D. card in explanation. In small print on the back appeared the following statements, 'Where more than two-thirds of a person's units are used up within a specified period (normally six months), additional units may be reallocated by the national authority. Units are interchangeable at a rate fixed from time to time in accordance with prevailing conditions. Variations will be made as necessary.'

Craig had assumed that additional units would be awarded according to need, at least to some degree. He was wrong.

The leggy secretaries and shapely female executives didn't stampede for Craig's body or company any more than had the schoolgirls and surfer chicks. Occasional initial enthusiasm was invariably followed by nonchalance and lack of interest. Although he listened hard to what the women said, he never seemed to grasp what they wanted and when they wanted it. The female employees tended to think of him as a nuisance or not to think of him at all. He had no close friends amongst the men either, as he never quite belonged, no matter what Craig said or did.

Periodically, this grade three clerk would escape the confines of his drab but frustrating work environment due to the occasional necessity for field trips. Despite the massive communications boom, sometimes the bureau would send employees out into the city at large to physically verify numbers. On April 3, Craig received instructions to check the statistics of all functions of the Regional Migrant Centre, including an actual head count and I.D. check of all persons there.

When he was about halfway through his task, Craig spotted a tall, stunningly beautiful Vietnamese girl watering some flower beds at the perimeter of an instruction hall. Perfectly symmetrical almond eyes were framed by faultless olive skin and long, shiny black hair. To him, she appeared as an Oriental goddess. Her eyes innocently laughed at him, and her lips parted into a half smile. The handsome young clerk was obliged to walk past the girl on his way to the next survey point. Fear of rejection or embarrassment had to be ignored as there was no choice. "Good morning. Nice flowers," ventured Craig as he drew level with the lass. As she was unable to speak the official language or English either, the girl smiled more deeply. The young man found himself responding in the same way. He showed his microcomputer and calculator by way of explanation for his presence. They exchanged names. Hers was Liu, Liu Tran Long. Craig offered some fruit he was carrying, and the smiling girl accepted. Liu showed him photographs of her family, while Craig demonstrated a noughts and crosses game with his calculator. He even made a joke using sign language, and Liu laughed aloud.

The encounter was brief due to the verification schedule. Four months elapsed. The smiling Asian beauty constantly featured in Craig's thoughts as he passed each day in his office prison. "Mr. Stephens," bellowed his immediate superior. "Come here!" His superior was more than angry. Craig had made a mistake in his verification figures, which was extremely unusual for him since he was completely in his element with numbers. He was given a stern warning and instructed to revisit the migrant center.

If they're not right this time, you'll lose more units than you could spend in a year!" boomed the boss. The shame Craig would normally have experienced was completely overshadowed by his joy at the chance of seeing the object of his dreams once more. He was out of the departmental building and across town in less than an hour.

Craig feverishly labored on his calculator in an inward, directional error search. Fortunately, he was able to guess where the mistake might lie. He found it quite quickly, which caused him considerable relief as he now had at least a spare hour and a half. He strode quickly to the compound where he had met the girl. There was no one in sight, but machine sounds accompanied by human voices emanated from the nearby instruction hall. Thirty-five minutes later, Liu appeared and, upon seeing him, came over, smiling as before. All her language skills were now at an acceptable level, and she would soon be allowed to leave the center. They spoke in English, but the important communication still came from the eyes. Craig asked for the address of her intended residence and suggested some outings together. Liu eagerly accepted, and Craig felt happy for the first time he could remember.

The clerk, a nuisance and a non-entity within the bureau, devoted all his leisure units and time to being with this girl from a strange and distant land. Even though Liu was a product of an alien culture, she seemed less remote, in a way that Craig couldn't understand, than the local girls he had known. "I always laughing when I see you," beamed Liu one evening. "I never know man like you before. Now I am happy." Craig recognized his feelings as those of love and realized they were reciprocated. He was beginning to genuinely comprehend the difference between real joy and illusion. The prison of his self was opening.

"Will you marry me?" Craig's question came with relative ease as he already knew the answer. A shadow appeared on Liu's lovely face before it was vanquished by her smile. "I love you with all my heart, but I not have Father's permission to marry you." Liu's eyes searched imploringly. "He in

Vietnam. He don't know Australia or Australians. Very different life there. I cannot marry without he saying 'yes,' and he no say 'yes.'" Liu kissed Craig and held him fast, but the young man was numb. "I understand," he replied. He softly kissed her good night and left.

Craig's depression was as sudden as it was real. His thoughts repeated themselves over and over in the same sequence. "Why? Why? Why? Asian prejudice against Europeans on the part of a foolish old man. How could a stranger destroy my only love for no reason?" How Craig wished he could become Vietnamese. He had never found any special happiness in being Australian. And now it had cost him his life's love. The morbid state of Craig's mind and the wretched condition of his feelings caused his work to suffer. There was no room for failures of this kind in modern Australia, and not even a hint of that room in government departments.

Against normal practice, the mathematics whiz whom nobody liked was allowed to resign despite his number of units being in a state of debit until all his holiday leave and twenty percent of his weekends were worked for a period of two years. Craig naturally had to vacate his cramped, state-owned bed- sitting room. With a negative tally of units, he couldn't afford to live anywhere. The last thing he did before he vanished was to send Liu a heart-wrenching letter. It told her that although he understood, he was too miserable to even see her anymore. Goodbyes said without anger or bitterness are the most pathetic and sad of all.

Craig was not only homeless; officially, he didn't even exist. People in his situation were somewhat of a rarity in the society governed by the Progressive Wealth Party. What few there were posed no problem for the authorities. They didn't have the means to commit any serious crimes, and they usually didn't live very long. They could eat from rubbish bins and sleep where they liked, provided they were not visible to the police or passersby. As long as they didn't cause an area to look untidy, they were simply ignored.

At least Craig was used to that. He drifted aimlessly for a week or so, then settled in a fairly private stormwater drain in Terrigal. He embarked on the serious business of drinking himself to death. Low-quality liquor was the only leisure item and one of the very few items of any category that didn't require any units. It was, in effect, free.

On reading Craig's last communication, Liu burst into a series of watery sobs, rolling down her face and dropping, one by one, onto another letter on her desk. It was in Vietnamese and was from her father. She had earlier written to him asking for permission to marry the man of her choice, the Australian Craig. Her father's letter not only gave permission but also conveyed the happy tidings that he had been accepted as an immigrant to Australia and would be leaving his homeland within two months.

The elegant girl with the almond eyes never abandoned hope of finding her love. She spent all of her free time searching the places most likely to be inhabited by the non-persons. It was another eight months before she found him. By this time, her spoken English was more than fluent. It had the grace and beauty which characterized the rest of her being. The dirty, rain-soaked form of Craig appeared before her in stark contrast. However, Liu's love was constant, and she lost no time embracing the pathetic, sorry figure and explaining his misunderstanding. She had never said that her father had forbidden her to marry Craig, merely that, as of that time, she hadn't asked or been granted his permission. "Everything will be all right now," thought the girl. They would soon be happy. To her surprise and horror, the man's eyes remained lifeless, and no smile appeared on his weather-beaten face.

It's too late," mumbled Craig, "I don't exist anymore. I not only don't have any credit units, I have negative units." He looked at the edge of the drain and then out to the distant breakers. "Don't you see there is no way we can be together? There is nothing for you to do but forget me."

When Liu learned of Craig's whereabouts, she called his old office in the bureau to discover his exact, official situation. The departmental head had given her a piece of computer paper in an envelope to deliver to Craig. He took it from her hand but didn't bother to open it. Surely, it was his official statement of unredeemed debt and declaration as a non-person. The bureau was like that. What he had thought was some sort of voluntary superannuation fund, the International Nest Egg Corporation, for which deduction of units were made on a regular basis, had proved to be a sham. How else could he have ended up with less than nothing?

They were both in tears by this time, but Liu insisted that he open the envelope. Mechanically, Craig extracted the paper and moved his dull eyes over the page.

"Craig Stephens. N° AF 4197782543 B. Grade 3 clerk. Winner 45 in Golden Nest Egg."

Gradually, Craig's eyes focused, and life appeared again on his face. He held Liu in his arms as if she were the only thing in the world. The Golden Nest Egg was a species of state lottery, not a superannuation fund, and against ridiculous odds, Craig had won. He wasn't going to become one of the mega-rich, but he was officially a person again with many credit units and had regained his lost love. He had been given a new start, the only start he really ever had.

Craig was no verbal genius, but he had the girl of his dreams. Maybe she would be good enough with words for both of them. Even if life wasn't meant to be easy, he possessed enough spare units to be able to buy a small sheep farm. Sheep don't verbalize too much, either.

The End

© 1989 John Spencer

The Reluctant Virgin

A couple of years ago, I was living in the central Philippines, and as a businessman, I often had the occasion to visit Manila. I would frequently call at "Chicks" bar, an establishment in the tourist area owned by a friend of mine. Richard was in his middle forties, and I was about ten years his junior. The bar featured loud music, cold beer, and about a dozen bikini-clad dancers. Although the dancers were very available and some were very beautiful, more often than not, I would pass the time simply in conversation or enjoying the odd free beer. One night, when I called in, I noticed a new girl who was charming but somewhat shy. I offered her a lady's drink and was given the reply, " No, thank you. I'm not thirsty." Sarah was her name, and we became quite friendly. Sarah was quite a pretty girl in her late teens and tall for a Filipina. She was obviously a total novice at her profession and didn't earn a great deal. I saw her a lot over the next few days, and she always appeared out of place there. Several times, I suggested to her that she might be better off thinking about changing her occupation, but she was adamant. Her other opportunities were few, and besides, she actually wanted to become a dancer. The hospitality industry, with its fast life, can seem glamorous to a young girl.

Sarah obviously liked me, but I had no desire to propel her along her chosen path. However, the girl was determined and twice she had left the bar with customers only to return in tears shortly afterward. She wanted to become a woman and experience many things but was afraid. For some reason she couldn't go forward but refused to return to her simple life. With tears in her eyes, Sarah asked me if I would pay her escort fee and take her to my hotel. She showed me a slip of paper that proved to be a doctor's certificate testifying to her virginity." How gauche," I thought to myself.

After she had assured me she really wanted this and wouldn't change her mind, I agreed. Once back in my room, I gingerly kissed her quivering lips. She responded, but she was afraid. "I'll go back to the bar now," she said. I explained to her that her sudden return there would cause me a loss of face and gently implored her to stay. Gradually, I won her confidence and helped her out of her garments. She was very shy and seemed reluctant to part with her faded cotton briefs. Sarah's physique was long and lean yet curved in all the right places. As she lay on the bed, my tongue tenderly caressed her nipples and flat stomach. She began to relax and allowed me to totally expose her nakedness. While my hands fondled Sarah's innocent behind and sleek thighs, I licked her navel and then sipped the satin skin below it. Her genital region was totally polished without a hair on it, yet it had obviously never been shaved. Parting her delicate inlet, I tasted her hidden flower with the tip of my tongue.

When I attempted to insert a finger, she stopped me. Sarah was still self-conscious and far from uninhibited. Her untried recesses were narrow, and it was no easy feat to introduce the head of my eagerly expectant member. Eventually, my hands firmly gripping the rounded orbs of Sarah's behind, I was able to push home through the natural obstruction of her maidenhead. With Sarah's love hole closed around my throbbing shaft, she was mine. The forbidden fruit tasted good. As she was experiencing some discomfort, I withdrew, and we both slept for a while. Telltale spots of blood on the linen confirmed the validity of her doctor's certificate. Upon awakening, we resumed our lovemaking. Although Sarah had been a virgin, I quickly unfurled a rubber over my already erect shaft to protect her from pregnancy and any fear she may have had of the monster virus. She was completely at ease now, and as I slipped my length into her waiting passage, the flow of her fragrant juices was matched by a soft moaning.

The sight of her hairless crotch enveloping my long caused my expectant cock to reach a thrusting frenzy. Firmly planted in Sarah's uncharted depths, it released a veritable flood of well-overdue male fluids while I fondled her enlarged clitoris. Her storm came moments later and was far from silent. Several days more of carnal love ensued, and when Sarah returned to her chosen profession, I wasn't sure if the world was ready.

The End

© John R. Spencer 1990

The Stalker

Joanne stirred her tea and gazed at her friend. "God, it's so good to see you after all this time. We've got so many things to catch up on." Barbara, a rather plain and plump lass, had been Joanne's closest friend at high school. That was seven years before Barbara moved away with her new job. Joanne was still gorgeous, only even more so. Her near-perfect figure had rounded out nicely, accentuating her sensual curves. Barbara rambled on about a succession of failed relationships, an unhappy marriage, and a financially successful divorce until Joanne "Speaking of that subject - MEN - Barb, did you hear about my terrible problem?" A shake of the head from the plain girl and, Joanne continued. "It was truly horrible. I've never been so terrified in all my life. For the past eighteen months or so, I've been the victim of one of those awful stalkers. You know, guys who write weird letters to you, ring you up all the time, and follow you everywhere."

"Yuk," sympathized Barbara, "unless he was good-looking." Joanne stared wistfully into her cup. "It's no joking matter. As a matter of fact, he was very handsome, but that's not the point. How would you like to get letters and phone calls day and night and have a stranger waiting and watching from the street?" Barbara reddened a little and remained silent.

"Every time I went to bed, I could feel eyes watching me through the gap in the curtains, and when I took a shower, I couldn't help but imagine the creep staring at my thighs, breasts, and that private place between my legs." Barbara looked tearful and showed genuine sympathy for her friend. "How did it all begin?" she inquired. "I don't really know," came the reply. "I received this letter on incredibly beautiful and expensive notepaper."

Joanne excused herself, rummaged in a nearby drawer, and returned, clutching a piece of pink stationery with an extremely loud, blue bow attached. Barbara read it with a mixture of nervousness and fascination.

Joanne, my love,

You first appeared to me in a dream. I saw your wavy brown hair, crystal blue eyes, and enchanting smile. A voice told me that you were mine. When you alighted from a train that day in the flesh, I knew the voice hadn't lied.

Your loving,

Ralph

"This is really creepy stuff," murmured Barbara excitedly. "What happened after that?"

"Oh, phone calls asking for dates, flowers on the doorstep; the usual. It was harmless enough at first. In fact, it was slightly flattering."

"Then what?" chirped the expectant Barbara.

A shadow passed over Joanne's face. "This guy kept catching the same train I did. Then I'd see him in the shopping mall. I guessed it was him! He then started to follow me sometimes, desperately trying to make it look like a coincidence. When I spotted him sitting in a car outside my house one morning on my way to work, I really freaked."

"Why didn't you call the cops?" asked Barbara with all the aplomb of a bush lawyer.

"I did," retorted her lovely friend, "but they said that unless he actually raped me or killed me or something, they couldn't do anything at all. Moreover, they told me that a restraining order against this jerk would be about as useful as a fridge in Antarctica."

"How did you protect yourself then?" cooed the genuinely concerned, plain, plump woman. Joanne looked a trifle confused.

"I added extra locks to my house and tried to change my appearance. I even bought a .22." "Heavy," came the mumble from across the coffee table.

"I even used it!" cried the gorgeous brunette. "One evening, he was just standing there, only twenty meters outside my front door. I fired two shots vaguely in his direction, but he came back again. And to make matters worse, one of the neighbors complained to the police, and they confiscated my rifle, saying that I was lucky to get off with only a warning."

"Holy shit!" exclaimed Barbara before she could stop herself. "It was totally hopeless," Joanne went on. "I thought about moving interstate, but I knew he'd find me. He was so confident of him- self that he even sent me a photograph and an account of his life's history. Quite sad, really."

"Then how on earth were you able to get rid of him?" questioned her earnest companion.

"I didn't," came the reply in a monotone. "He's still in my life to this very day!"

"How awful!" exclaimed Barbara while quietly thinking that she'd better leave as soon as possible,

At that moment, heavy footsteps echoed on the patio, and the front door handle turned.

"It's him!" cried Joanne. The door swung open, and there stood an incredibly handsome man.

"Barbara, I'd like you to meet my husband, Ralph. He's a really sweet guy once you get to know him, just a little shy, that's all."

The End

© 1994 John Spencer

<u>Salubrious white collar smoos</u>

I've finally made it. Success, respect, and wealth have finally found me. As a company director, I'm SHOWN to my new office with plush carpets, a stylish bar, a state-of-the-art computer and printer, and TWO ABSOLUTELY LUSCIOUS SECRETARIES. A blonde of nineteen and an equally curvaceous brunette in her late twenties sit CROSS LEGGED on dainty stools, the hems of their smart mini slicking at their SUCCULENT THIGHS.

"Good morning, Sir," they chorus. "We are here to attend to ALL your needs." Before I can even sit down at my desk, the blonde unzips my fly and proceeds to demonstrate her prowess at

DICKTATION. My throbbing member is at full stretch in a corporate

SALUTE as she continues, simultaneously discarding her work clothes. AS IF I wasn't distracted enough from mundane commercial duties already the brunette drops her skirt and panties and sits on my desk, her back propped up against the computer screen. Her proud breasts BREAK FREE of her business shirt, and her fine black bush addresses me at eye level. She demands a TONGUE LASHING and begs for a bit of SHORTHAND as well. The moist triangle between her legs then craves for some INPUT from the boss, and I willingly <u>oblige. The office temperature is TOO MUCH for the air conditioning, which gives up with a groan. Meanwhile, the blonde, standing by, complained that she didn't like long tea breaks and demanded equal WORK TIME. Breaking from the black-haired girl I turn to</u>

the blonde, APPRECIATING HER MANY TALENTS. Smallish but well-shaped hills with tight nipples stand guard over an ASHEN FOREST, almost hiding her LOVE TUNNEL. The rounded cheeks of her contoured backside wiggle from side to side as she awaits FURTHER INSTRUCTIONS.

MAKING MY POINT, I deliver my REPORT very moistly as she straddles her own chair. The INS and OUTS of life at the top increase in PACE while the elder secretary presents her EXCITED BEAVER for ORAL discussion.

<u>The computer groans, the printer clatters, and the secretaries</u>

MOAN, when the door opens, and the Office girl ENTERS. Complaining about discrimination and mumbling something about EQUAL OPPORTUNITY, she DIVES into the action. Life at the top just gets busier and BUSHIER.

The End

© 1994 John Spencer

Life of a Manila Prostitute

It was already midday. She opened her eyes, trying to remember where she was. The snoring form of the unshaven naked man next to her soon refreshed her memory. She woke him and asked for the money. "I have to go home now," she mumbled in a monotone. The man reached into the pocket of his trousers lying on the dresser and produced six hundred pesos. Throwing her clothes on and heading for the door, almost in one action, she departed. Last night, the girl had been lucky. The man was rather drunk and not in the mood for too much action and had been generous. As long as she hadn't caught anything, she considered herself to have done well. It was a half-hour jeepney ride from the hotel to her rented room in the squatter area, but she didn't have to work again until seven, and she could rest for a bit.

The girl could have been any one of thousands plying the clubs and bars of the capital. A pretty face and a good body had been her only opportunity, and she hadn't been slow to use them. Manila has a countless number of hostesses, dancers, and masseuses willing to sell their physical endowments. Through the eyes of just three girls, we can understand the situation of many.

Vivian works in an expensive club in Pasay, one of a dozen or so catering almost exclusively to foreign tourists. She came from a poor family living in a shanty town in Cebu, the second biggest city in the Philippines and some six hundred kilometers south of Manila. She had received some schooling, third-year high school, in fact, and like many girls in her situation, she could speak good English. Her parents considered that they had more than done their duty to her and now wanted something in return. Vivian was the eldest of ten children, and her parents were also fond of drinking and celebrating fiesta neighborhood parties. With unemployment running at forty percent, to look for a job without a college education was a waste of time. Her mother would sell cigarettes and sweets to earn a few pesos, while her father intended to start a small business if only he could raise the necessary capital. He was sure his luck at betting on the cockfights would change. It was a poor thing to always back a loser when there were only two contestants.

Vivian faced a lot of pressure to earn money. Then there was that scandal when she was fifteen. Her boyfriend had professed undying love and seduced her, only to run away. She hadn't become pregnant, but the affair had been the talk of the neighborhood, and nobody was going to let her forget. "Men are so unfair," she often thought. Finally, her parents paid her boat fare and sent her to Manila to work as a domestic servant. "Remember, we are counting on you," her papa had said. Her mother expected her to send home two thousand pesos a month, conveniently forgetting that the average maid's salary was only six hundred. Even shop assistants only earned twelve hundred, and then they had to pay for their accommodation and food.

She had tears in her eyes as the ship pulled out from the dock, and her brothers and sisters waved. That was three years ago. Vivian was now twenty years old. She had been recruited to work in the body trade within a week of arriving in Manila. She had... changed bars a few times but liked the upmarket appearance of the one in Pasay. She would start work at eight in the evening and dance until three. If she was sick or took a day off, she received no pay.

The girls enter the stage in groups of thirty. Every twenty minutes the group would change so the dancing wasn't tiring. She had been shy at first to stand up before so many men, wearing nothing but the briefest of bikinis. Now she was used to it, and since she had a good body with shapely breasts, slender legs, and a cute little backside, she thought, "Why shouldn't I display it?" To be admired by so many men was wonderful. There was also the camaraderie with the other girls. It was fun to show off new clothes or jewelry that a customer had given. Of course, it was difficult to stop a lot of the girls from stealing anything too pretty or valuable.

If a customer fancied her, he would have her call over by number and buy her a drink, usually a soft drink for which he would pay P150. They would sit at a table and indulge in the usual small talk. Vivian's number was twenty-three, and it was called quite often. For dancing, she was paid ninety pesos a night and received fifty for each drink a customer bought her. Often, that was as far as things would go. Sometimes, however, two or three times a week on average, a customer would ask her for more. He would then pay a bar fine of P400 to the establishment and take her to pay for his hotel. She would get nothing from the four hundred but would expect the customer to give her at least that much the following morning.

If a customer were too old, Smelly, or didn't look rich enough, she would sometimes refuse to go with him, but she couldn't do that too often. The manager would become angry and threaten to fire her. Besides, she really needed that extra money. Her rent for a small, broken-down room in Paco cost P600 a month, and then she had to eat. The club would give the girls health checks twice monthly and deduct the P100 cost from their salary.

Safe sex was unheard of in this neck of the woods until quite recently, but even now, many of the men refused to use condoms, and the customer was always right. Besides, the Catholic Church said that birth control was a sin, and she surely didn't want to go to hell. If a customer took her out more than once, Vivian referred to him as her boyfriend. At last count, she had six regular "boyfriends."

Usually, when she went out on a "bar fine," she would spend the night in some seedy little room. However, sometimes, the clients were more affluent, and she had slept in every five-star hotel in Manila at one time or another. Once, a customer had taken her for a week's holiday in Puerta Galera. It had been enjoyable staying in a cottage by the beach, that was until the man took a liking to another girl there and dumped her. She had had to make her own way back to the capital. Every year, Vivian would go home for Christmas and spend a week with her family. It was fun but expensive because of all the presents she had to buy. Now, of course, she also had to send more money home than before. One client had given her more than she had bargained for. A fatherless baby was another expense and one more problem. Her parents weren't exactly filled with grand paternal pride either.

Candy's introduction to life as a prostitute in Manila was more sudden and a more brutal shock than had been Vivian's. She was now twenty-one. She was not quite seventeen when 'her stepmother brought her into a small, tidy little bar in the heart of the tourist belt.

Candy's childhood had been a simple but happy one. Her father, who loved her deeply, had put her right through high school and her existence had been carefree enough. That was before her mother died and her father remarried. Her stepmother had never liked her. Still, her loving father ensured she was cared for. Then, a year before her entry into the bar, her daddy was murdered while driving a taxi. The culprits were never found. Life became harder, all the more so because her demanding stepmother blamed her for all their misfortunes. She had no brothers or sisters and felt alone in the world. The stepmother had begun gambling and would often beat her. Candy would cry herself to sleep at night and had visibly become depressed and nervous.

In her endless search for the money to sustain her gambling and penchant for younger men, Agria, the stepmother, would stop at nothing. She was a plain woman of fifty, and cash was her only chance. All the tears in the world did not dissuade her. A neighbor had told her about the easy money in the tourist belt, and without much hesitation she literally dragged Candy into "Flirtations" to begin work.

Candy was still sixteen, a virgin, and very frightened. However, the owner of the nightclub, an elderly Australian man, was kind and did not force her to go out with customers. She didn't even have to dance; she merely accepted ladies' drinks and talked with the patrons. However, the owner's girlfriend, known as the Dragon Lady, was not so softhearted.

Lurna, as she was addressed, thought she could get a high price for a virgin from one of the Middle Eastern or Japanese customers. Still, the owner was a little protective.

Candy had only been there a week or so when one of the owner's friends visited Manila and called in. He was tall, handsome, and softly spoken. She liked him a lot. He wasn't pushy, and she went willingly when he invited her to stay with him because she trusted him. He had been a true gentleman the first few nights and had not tried anything. Yet men are always men. When the moment finally happened, it had been painful, and she cried. After a couple of days, her lover had left, promising to return, and she went back to the bar, although he had given her plenty of money and asked her not to.

No sooner had his plane taken off than a young businessman from India was seated next to Candy and buying her drinks. He liked her shy innocence and desperately wanted to try a virgin. Candy did not want to go with him, and she was no longer a virgin for that matter. Lurna, the Dragon Lady, had other ideas. She had guaranteed the visitor of the girl's innocence and would sell her cheaply' at only P10,000. Candy hated the idea but was scared of Lurna, who had friends in the police, and the kind owner was not there that night. Thus, she was forced into acting the part and living a lie. She was now firmly entrenched in a profession from which there is seldom a turning back.

Three weeks later, she was the subject of a bout of jealousy and a fistfight between two friends in a hotel room. That was ugly and embarrassing. From that point on, her life was like that of the other girls: lies, deceptions, and three or four nights a week of sleeping with different men. She did get to like the money, while her stepmother had died from a heart attack.

Candy was now working for herself. At twenty-one, her life was the same: the endless round of hotels and the occasional "holiday" with a client. One week a young German had taken her for a few days holiday to Dakak, a very expensive (in fact an overly expensive) beach resort in northern

Mindanao. While eating breakfast one morning on the outdoor terrace, she glanced at the table opposite. There was the man who had deflowered her all those years before. He didn't approach, and she didn't speak. She just stared.

Nora's story is similar to Candy's, with a different twist. Her parents had died when she was young, and she was raised in Laguna by a not-so-favorite aunty. The aunty had heard about the rich pickings from the hospitality industry and had introduced her to a nightclub in central Manila. Nora was sixteen and also a virgin. The owner had taken her to a doctor who had issued a dated certificate to testify to the fact. Night after night, her aunty entered the bar to ask for the money. Nora was dancing and had twice gone out with customers only to return a few minutes later in tears and still intact. Yet she swore she was determined to be a hostess. After all, it was the only chance she had to make a reasonable living. There was also always the possibility that a foreigner might marry her and take her out of the Philippines.

It didn't work out like that, though. The first man she slept with, whom she had real feelings for, had not given her a great amount of money. Her aunty, known as the crocodile because of her capacity to turn on tears over a few pesos, was enraged. Nora had had to sleep with as many men as possible to make enough money to keep her aunt satisfied. Several years later she was still plying her trade and also had a son to support.

In all probability, Vivian, Candy, and Nora are still working as prostitutes somewhere in Manila. Their stories demonstrate sadness, misfortune, foolishness, and the addictive quality of the lifestyle they entered. No amount of money would satisfy their relatives and it is doubtful if they themselves find their lifestyles happy and satisfying.

The End

© 1994 John Spencer

<u>Typical</u>

She had a face like a goddess and a slender, sensual body that provoked desire. Shoulder length, jet black hair licked full, rounded bosoms while her slender waist gave way to powerful but sleek thighs and an exquisitely contoured backside. Night after night, she did her stuff, pounding the stage to the rhythm of a wanton, "sexually lost" disco beat. In a secondary part of Manila, she waited for her chance, like so many other girls. But Nora was different. To start with, she was dragged there by her aunty, whom the neighbors affectionately called "the crocodile." On top of that, she was only sixteen, a real sixteen, not one born of believing customers and too many drinks. And then, she was a virgin. Therein lay the dilemma. Rich Japanese tourists and the odd 'sheik' from the Middle East would offer to help her out in her new profession, but Nora was no fool. She had a lot to sell and would sell it if the price was right. No cheap hustlers were going to invade her lotus.

Being a very young girl, she had made a few false starts. Twice, in fact, she had been persuaded that 'tonight was the night' only to return thirty minutes later in tears and a virgin still. The owner of the bar and the grunty little manager were not impressed. This was bad for business. Word would get around. A real virgin for sale is very nice, but one that runs away from the burning bed faster than an outclassed fireman was a definite no-no. This sort of thing didn't happen in Tokyo, Jeddah, Melbourne, or Wellington, for that matter (but for different reasons). Therefore, Nora's unseen pussy remained inviolate.

The ritzy door swung open, and stumbling down the step, a slightly less than sober Australian entered. Tall, with a tan, he wasn't bad looking and possessed a veneer of class that so many of the patrons lacked. He had been there before; in fact, he was known. 'Captain Nobody, ' the bar owner called him. All the girls wondered why he would come and go so often and how he could afford to drink so much. Even when drunk, he didn't talk too much and gave nothing away. More surprisingly, he didn't take any of the girls out.

Naturally, 'Gormless,' as the manager called Nora when he dared to speak, was besotted with the newcomer. She wiggled her sensual arse and shook her upper endowments a little more than usual when he was looking her way. Jack was polite but cool. He could look at flesh all night long and keep his trousers straight. Nothing phased this bastard. Five nights after she had first laid eyes on him, Nora was perched on the next stool, sipping on the first ladies' drink Jack had bought in a year. Nora was pleasant, after all, despite being a crash-hot piece of arse.

The regular small talk was brief and irrelevant. "Who are you?" the sixteen-year-old virgin asked, and "Why are you here?" Jack just smiled. "What do you think?" he muttered. The disco beat got louder. "Boom, boom, boom; back to my room." The virgin had no idea. "I'm in the information business," mumbled the tall Aussie, downing the last mouthful of a San Miguel. "CIA?" ventured Nora in her innocence. Everybody within earshot laughed, including the recipient.

While Jack was briefly in the Men's room, another dancer informed the sixteen-year-old that her companion was somehow connected with the Australian government. Australia is a long way from Manila, mentally, if not in terms of distance. When Jack returned, Nora told him her story of poverty, misery, and crocodiles. She knew that the intoxicated form next to her was her ticket out. There was no denying it. Cool as any man might be, her body, with its untried promise, could not fail.

When Jack paid the bar fine, the owner and the insipid manager were both smiling in unison. The girl would learn her trade at last. Neither of them knew that this particular customer was a very important man. The maiden with the showcase loins donned her clothes and hesitantly stepped onto the street. Stepping over the usual putrescent garbage and into a taxi, she held her breath. The vehicle pulled up at a modest, somewhat plain hotel. "This guy must be really important," she mused. "A five-star hotel would be a giveaway."

Nora liked Jack, but cowardice got the better of her. Ten minutes after arriving and seconds after his passionate kiss planted itself on her mouth, she begged to go back. With his foot firmly planted against the door, the Australian explained that such an action would be an embarrassment to a person like him and, therefore, she must go through with it. The simple cotton shirt was removed, and the blue jeans followed suit. The virgin was naked save for a pair of white cotton panties. Her breasts heaved nervously but in vain. As the government man ripped off her knickers, he was surprised by what he saw. A sleek, smooth, and succulent vagina but not a trace of pubic hair. A virgin with a virgin twat! Like all of us, he thought such things only existed in movies or as a result of shaving. Nora gasped. The pain was unbearable as her maidenhood gave up. The evidence of her loss would embarrass the hotel staff, surely. But she had made it. She knew he cared for her, and he was a government man. At last, she would be free!

Every time they made love, it still hurt, but at least the pain was tolerable now. She told him she loved him and had obliged with tears and blood to prove the point. When he left that day for the airport, Nora was crying uncontrollably. Sure, she wanted to escape. Who wouldn't? But she had really come to love him. The two of them could be happy in that far-off land to the south. With a heavy heart, she returned to the bar. While accepting the countless ladies' drinks offered and their scant commission, she steadfastly refused to go with any of the customers. The dour-faced owner of the bar and the weaselly manager were quite disappointed. It was just like an expensive yearling that couldn't win a race.

Jack didn't return. They knew he wouldn't. Yet, their star performer wouldn't perform. There was only one strategy left. They would tell her the truth. And so, they did. Jack was a government man, all right. He was almost wanted. He had gone to university with the son of the leader of the Communist Party and was, therefore, marked for life. Not only that, but he had been in jail for non-payment of parking fines. The mere mention of his name could close a government office.

Nora's scream echoed from Rizal Park to Quezon City. Not only had she parted with her most precious possession for nothing, but also, she was getting older. She had hit seventeen. There was nothing left to do.

The owner and the reptilian manager smiled at last. Outside, a minibus full of Japanese executives in search of virgins had just pulled up.

The End

(c) John Spencer 1994

The Underpants and the Chandelier.

How not to score despite seemingly foolproof odds.

Between the lines of every heartrendingly tragic saga lurk the seeds of advice. After all, part of self-esteem involves being one-up on the next guy. Read on carefully, and your own love life should multiply in a biblical sense. As a fellow Aussie, Peter, my long-time accomplice in the "go forth" epic, knew only too well the misery associated with the sexual drought. Sure, we'd both been to Asia, but we had to live in downtown suburban Oz out of economic necessity, didn't we?

Sydney being a big place and our general sphere of operations, we had for many years devised a geographical approach. In a military-type fashion, our map of bars, discos, and clubs was divided into all the segments of the compass. The north and east sides had yielded only limited potential, but in one year, like a fresh breeze, came the word: "South and southwest!" That's where the girls outnumbered the guys and where their defenses would be weakest."

Accordingly, one Tuesday night, we headed off due south in my fading, twenty-year-old vehicle. Both being on holiday, we could give the task in hand our best shot. It was winter, and the first bar we selected boasted several roaring log fires and relaxed, boring music. Our research appeared to be correct: not much opposition, and quite a few attractive girls clustered in small groups.

Next to one very cozy hearth were standing two sexy but bored-looking girls, the taller one dressed in a clinging dress of white wool and the other sporting a pale crimson skirt and heavy silver coat. "You're the one with the mouth," Peter muttered. "Do your stuff." My request for space next to the flames for two frozen males was met with a friendly response. Jill and Jacky were apparently sales girls for a large department store, and they announced quite definitely that they had come there to listen to the nondescript music.

"Why did you come?" questioned Jill, her clinging woolen dress clinging a little more fervently. "Oh, we are school teachers forcing ourselves to enjoy our holidays." My reply sounded a little lame, even to my own ears. Although definitely interested, these girls seemed to lack the sympathetic understanding that can make a conquest easy. What the hell! We weren't going to be daunted by little problems of the human spirit. The woolen dress seemed to get tighter by the second, and her friend's coat had long since been removed, revealing a bust line that was very much alive.

With the confidence enhanced by the drinks and the warm caress of the fire, it was time to make our invitation. "I know it's already late," I gushed, "and you girls have to work tomorrow, but we couldn't leave without inviting you for coffee." The catch was that we lived more than thirty kilometers from either the bar or their houses. "The northern beaches are always worth a visit, regardless of the hour of day or time of year." Perhaps, slightly to my surprise, my hollow words met with no opposition whatsoever.

It was agreed. We made an exit from the bar as graciously as possible, bundled the girls into the car, and headed north along General Holmes Drive and then over the Harbor Bridge. Jill was an exceptionally pretty brunette with a smooth complexion and was to be my paramour for the coffee. Her accomplice was an attractive blonde who had already overcome Peter's slight reserve. Both Peter and I lived in apartments of which we were the sole occupants. His perhaps had a greater charm than mine, was culturally endowed with numerous works of art, and was spotlessly maintained. It had, however, one fundamental disadvantage: only one bedroom.

Accordingly, I drove the car into my own familiar driveway. The whole journey had been one of happiness, at least on my part. I had engaged in the not-too-intellectually strenuous small talk, secure in the knowledge that only the sweet, sticky smell of success can give.

"We must be a hell of some guys," I thought, "to be able to convince two such beautiful strangers to accompany us for more than thirty kilometers at such an hour on a weeknight." The subject of coffee was the furthest thing from my mind as our little foursome strode into the hallway of my apartment. Nothing could go wrong now. The clinging white dress was going to be mine. The rain had come to the desert at last. And Jacky was so enamored of my friend that she wouldn't have noticed if we had brought her to hell.

However, the newfound springtime that had just settled on the heart of this suburban boy had neglected to consider Murphy's law. As we entered my abode, the object of my passion was keenly surveying the sights around her. The woolen dress seemed to cling a little less. Never mind the -carpet and a certain amount of residual dust on the walls. After all, great lovers like great artists don't have the time to attend to such mundane things. But there, hanging from the chandelier, like a message from God, was a pair of my underpants. Contrary to the folk story that this sight later inspired, the underpants had been previously washed and were merely there to dry.

My sweet Jill was beginning to look just a little like a frozen beauty. Even her friend disengaged herself from Peter's embrace and looked around. My lovely brunette then promptly demanded the coffee that I had promised her. "White with two sugars, please," she said definitely, the sign of a girl who knows her own mind. A hasty sortie into the kitchen revealed a ghastly truth. "Not only was there no sugar or milk; there wasn't even any coffee. Not one to be daunted, I quickly waltzed all my guests around the piles of clothing and books on the floor and placed them in dusty armchairs.

"Coffee isn't really that good for you, you know?" I mumbled. "Anyone for Bonox, beef drink." Two outraged female faces and one miserable male countenance stared up at me from the dusty armchairs. "I don't believe this," echoed Jill's voice as she strode directly to the phone and rang for a taxi. At this point, her friend distanced herself from Peter and joined her. Two or three minutes of silence followed, then the honk of the cab, and finally, the two objects of our hopes and dreams marched down the stairs and out of our lives forever. Against all odds, I had singlehandedly snatched defeat from the jaws of victory.

The failed Don Juan is seldom a gentleman. There was no way I was going to be chivalrous and save the girls the cab fare by driving them home. "The driver probably needs the money," I mused as I sat there directly below the underpants and tried not to notice the wrathful gaze of my friend.

The End

© John Spencer 1994

Murphy's Choice

Al Roberts' internal choir was humming 'Shanghai-ed by a Chinese lady' and 'Shaken down in China town' as he struggled through the smog-laden streets of Taipei with his luggage. At almost thirty-nine years of age, he found himself working for virtually nothing designing travel brochures on a contract basis. At least he got to travel.

The maniacal traffic of that particular city seemed to threaten him individually. He was tired, and the closest he had ever come to communicating in Chinese was waving a chopstick in a Chinese restaurant. The latest edition travel guide had just directed him to a flea pit of a hotel that no longer existed. Another inauspicious day in an inauspicious life. Al's head was slightly more peaceful than the buzzing of countless motorcycles as he approached the nearest, not-too-expensive lodgings. The name of this not very impressive structure, when translated into English, read as 'Rises again.' Mr. Roberts paid an advance and dragged his baggage up to the third floor after a minute or two's reflection on the meaning of names. The next day, he commenced his work. He had to work hard for it, and although he didn't know it, the first day of his last chance had begun.

Al was always a little strange. He was the last child in his class to learn the alphabet. He wasn't good enough to be on the football team, and as for the school choir, that was absolutely out of the question. Nor was he ever allowed to play the drums for the parade. Furthermore, he was always a little late for school and could never quite manage the expected standard of dress when wearing his uniform. Yet untalented he was not, just strange, and perhaps it bothered him a little.

Although a pleasant enough-looking young man, Al's formative years followed the same pattern. The girls liked him, but nothing much ever came of it. He was a good student, and there, and only there, did he hold his own. With a good education behind him, he pursued a career in computing. He did not know what was missing. The machines may not have objected to the occasional strangeness, but in that regard, they were alone.

Strange feelings gave rise to strange thoughts, and the sunlight moved out of the world. If a girl smiled the wrong way, a torment would eat at his consciousness, and a misplaced thought or feeling would have all the power of black magic. The damned computers he worked with appeared to look wrong. In time, the young man's mind resembled an emotional and intellectual battlefield.

'Recovery always takes time in cases like this. You'll see.' The professionals in the white coats had been very kind and done all they could. Therapy had only turned Al into a legal drug addict. A bottle of whisky a day had at least been able to bring a temporary armistice to the mind on occasion. However, with a future no longer than the next armed and dangerous feeling or thought, even the distillers of Kentucky couldn't have been optimistic in this case.

What followed was Al's first real taste of Asia: the flashing smiles and deadly curves of the angels of Bangkok and their sisters in Manila. The neon glintze and throbbing disco music fought side by side with the private demons in Al's mind to be heard. Either the music or the madness screamed 'love,' and Al found himself back in New York State with a piranha whose feelings for Al extended no further than her plane ticket, visa, and future bank account. A few years, one child and an expensive divorce later, Al found himself starting again, handicapped but with clearer thoughts.

In the way of the world, the wish of death makes repeat visits. Al's second choice was a small improvement on the first. Lisa, unlike her predecessor, whose origins coincidentally were only two city blocks from her own, could at least be pleasant. As they said in her social circles, 'Age doesn't matter, and love can be developed.'

The more ridiculous they are, the more popular and often quoted common lies tend to be. A familiarity and even a fondness can perhaps grow over time, but not love, surely not that. Yet, one is out of sync. The world seems to try anything, if not on purpose, then by accident. Al rented a dingy little apartment in a suburb of the Philippines' second-largest city. There, he had the best of both worlds. Someone to come home to, the sweetness of the flesh when he needed it, but not a wife as such, with the ferocity and quickness to complain normally associated with the lady of a house. Married when he needed to be but otherwise as single as a lark on a sunny day, Al threw his body and soul into the fulfillment of tropical dissolution.

"Where you been?" Lisa would sometimes scowl as Al crossed the doorstep, the fragrance of beer and lipstick still upon him. The reply would be either "Roaming around" or merely a smile. She had to be satisfied with this as there was no other choice. The time when he had brought a "dancer" home and forgotten that Lisa had been there had resulted in screams, the crashing of pans across the walls, and death threats but nothing more. Then there was the day of the accident. Al's motorcycle had crashed into a cement block on a city street in the hours of darkness, and he had ended up in hospital. "But who was the sexy girl who had been his pillion passenger, and why was she with him?" Lisa's question was soon answered. Maria, although only slightly injured, was placed in the same private hospital room with Al. Despite the injury to his right leg, even in hospital he was given the opportunity to pander to his weaknesses.

"You must give seventy-five percent of all your property to your wife," the judge in the divorce court had said. Rachael, the vulture who had first got hold of Al, had begun the process of taking him down. Of course, she got the child. She would soon have more than that. She would have everything that there was to have. Rachael knew her rights and where to find a slippery lawyer to help her enforce them. Al never knew why she hated him so much; surprising, really, when one considers that she had never loved him or even liked him. "Hell hath no fury like a woman deprived of a free meal ticket, perhaps," mused the odd man. Strange he was, but not stupid. Before the judge could even wink at his ex-wife Al had sold every asset he possessed and transferred all the funds to his tropical paradise. Fortunately, all his property was in his name, and he was very quick to dispose of it.

Back once more with his comfortable life and comfortable Lisa in the land of a million palm trees and an oppressive heat that never dissipated, Al decided to settle down a little. He bought an attractive Spanish-style house in a good suburb and pursued his business as a B-grade, travel-advertising man with renewed vigor. He learned even to be a little more discreet with the joys of dissipation. He moderated his habit of overly quenching his thirst ever so slightly, and it was seldom that Lisa found any tangible evidence of womanizing.

Lisa became pregnant, and life was more restrained. Yet the demands of anticipated business success soon necessitated hiring a secretary. Hilary was Lisa's cousin, a college graduate in her late twenties. She worked well and was a good manager. Still, the strange man's precarious business never seemed to prosper. Later that year, Al took Lisa to the States to visit his family. While there, she had become very ill and was forced to remain when he returned. Their daughter, "Princess," was born while he was away.

The new secretary, Hilary, was more than an efficient employee for Al; she was a good friend. She understood his moods and problems and was a valuable confidant. More than that, she was physically attractive, and Mr. Robert's thoughts couldn't help but notice her shapely curves, proud but modestly attired breasts, and thighs that reeked of an urgent, though innocent sexuality. Hilary, likewise, seemed attracted to Al.

It had been on a business trip to Manila, with just the two of them alone in their hotel room, that matters developed to the point where trouble undoubtedly would be sown for the future. "Lay me down," the shapely Hilary had said as she lay on the bed, clad only in a pair of white lace panties. Their embraces and kisses were passionate and steamy, burning with desire, yet Hilary would not allow Al to do the deed. From that time on, their relationship became one of tantalizing frustration as well as friendship and business. "You want me, I want you," Al would often implore. "Why not?"

"Lisa is my cousin, and it's wrong," Hilary would moan between kisses and sensual caresses that shot fire through both of them. However, the temptation was always there. Night after night, she would come to his bed quietly so that no one else could hear. Always, at the last possible second, she would pull back. "Not by this time," she would say in answer to Al's urgent entreaties.

One hot night after the typhoon and the month-long electricity failure that had followed, Hilary lay down next to Al. Often, they would both be naked, yet she would still escape. This night was different. The heat and the stillness, added to interminable frustration, resulted in a greater determination. Through the soft sounds of insincere protests, their sexual relationship had been consummated. In every sense of the word, they were lovers, associates, and friends. They needed each other physically, emotionally, and in every conceivable way. Still, however, Hilary would resist further acts of consummation. "Was she intrinsically frightened of the sex act itself?" Al would often ask himself and sometimes her, but to no avail. The sexual game of cat and mouse continued over considerable periods of time. Al would spend months back home with Lisa and Princess, but he would always return. His business was still losing money, but that unpleasant fact never stopped him. Countless nights and days, the frustration of his time with Hilary in their burning palace would tell on them both.

He offered to marry her, but she refused because of the shame such a thing would cause. "Not by this time," came the unfaltering reply. "I'll bring you to the U.S., and we'll be happy," Al promised. "What'll everybody think of me if I do that to my cousin?" came the response. Thus, the situation lingered like a storm frozen in time. Neither of them could let go, but neither could resolve their passion, love, and fear. Kisses in the dark and passion in the kitchen. Such was the course of secret love. A quick, forceful touch, a lingering caress of a searching hand, would break the respectable monotony if no one was around.

This was the situation when Al accepted an assignment to write brochures for the tourist industry in Taipei. A life that was going nowhere, either economically or personally. He slept in the boring little hotel and had dutifully commenced work the next morning. All day, he trudged from business to business, returning in the middle of the evening. On entering his hotel, he noticed something that was not the same. The desk clerk was different. A beauty with long, flowing raven hair smiled at him with penetrating eyes.

He introduced himself and asked the girl her name. "My name Ming Wong Wai," she laughed, "but sorry, I no speak English." She smiled at him so hard that Al became uncomfortable, excused himself, and disappeared up the stairs. Almost every afternoon and evening, she would be sitting there. She was there when he came home from work. She was there when he went out to dinner and likewise when he came back again. He had the greatest of difficulties remembering her name, so she finally offered "Grace" as her English name. Sometimes, she would talk a little, but mostly, she just smiled and stared. Grace's English was better than she claimed, but generally, a ten-minute conversation was all Al could bear. He felt so damned uncomfortable without knowing why. He knew he should stay away from this girl but was drawn to her. He couldn't guess her age, but she was obviously too young for him, so there wasn't going to be a problem. If he did succumb and make some kind of advance, she would merely laugh at him, and he would feel foolish.

One evening, he returned quite late, and she was just finishing her shift. "Can I tempt you with a cup of coffee before you go home?" he remarked with a casual innocence that would protect his fragile ego from any embarrassment. To his surprise, Grace accepted the invitation, and the two of them found themselves sitting in an almost deserted nearby coffee house.

"Must be honest, "the Chinese beauty had said as they sat down. "What a strange thing to say," Al thought, yet he felt a squirm inside.

They had talked of many things. Life, love, people, and even the future and what it could all mean. Mr. Roberts did not talk about the past, of Lisa, of Hilary, or of the wretched Rachael and her senseless, silent vow to destroy him and his. "How could one talk of such things to such a sweet, innocent girl? Besides an age, a culture and a language gap made such verbal horror impossible."

At the end of an hour, when he returned to the hotel, and Grace had gone home, Al realized why he had always felt uncomfortable in her presence and why she had seemed to stare at him so much. It wasn't the common binding of friendship or the idle fancy of a young girl. What had occurred was that rare thing with the power to save or to destroy; a thing that there is no running away from. Al was changed forever, but still, he did not realize it.

A month later, after a trip to Laos, Al returned to the shabby little hotel and to the girl with the smiling eyes. The speed and intensity of their love affair surprised them both. Against all her strict upbringing and habit, Grace could not refuse him, and on Al's part, his previous discomfort was suddenly replaced with a naturalness and ease that didn't even occur in his dreams. What had transpired was beyond a dream. Funny how life's cruel mockery had presented him with the love he had always wanted in a situation and time in his life where he could not have it.

On the day he left, confusion and a vague sense of loss reigned in his soul. All he could do was promise to return, a promise he fully intended to keep and one which he indeed kept. Back with his Hilary, the frustration and nightly encounters continued. It seemed he loved both women but yet was bound to another. He returned to Taipei for a fortnight. Grace was as before but only more so. By now, he knew his heart had been touched forever. Yet still, the living specter of his lovely secretary and her deadly game haunted him. "Did Hilary really love him? If so, why would she not surrender herself completely? If not, then why had she stayed so close to him for all these years in the face of difficult circumstances?"

After returning to the States, two women constantly occupied his thoughts while he lay in the bed of a third. Life with Lisa was comfortable enough, and God knew how much he loved little Princess. Al received love letters from both his darlings, not that Lisa ever found them. Yet there was an urgency in those from Grace that penetrated Al's spirit. He would have to return to the girl with the smiling eyes. The only way he could engineer this, given his financial difficulties, was to return to the Philippines with Lisa and Princess and then go alone from there to Taiwan for a "work" opportunity.

Back in the smoggy grounds of Taipei once more, he was happy in Grace's arms. Yet a mystery remained between them. "I know you have some secret from me," the Chinese girl would often say. Many times, Al tried to tell her, but the words choked in his throat. He knew what they had with each other but was terrified of losing it. He had confessed the story of his first marriage and how that harpy had haunted his steps ever since. Grace's reaction was such that he had been unable to say anything more.

Still, the two or so months that they were able to spend together before their next parting had been a wonderful time. Picnics in the winter sunshine, all kinds of adventures together, and the warmth of each other's passion had truly cemented their love. Both knew that, somehow, this had to be forever. Otherwise, what meaning lay in life?

Back once more in the white mansion under the palm trees of endless summer, but this time with both Lisa and Hilary under the same roof, Al's nemesis began its steady, unrelenting approach. He seemed to have grown slightly apart from his sexy friend, and the need for utmost secrecy and discretion was now paramount. Yet there was still that bond between them that would explode into passion at the slightest opportunity. Lisa was the same, and Princess could always make Al smile. Still, the ache in his heart for his little China girl grew into a pain he couldn't ignore. Hilary knew of

Grace's existence, but Lisa knew nothing of Al's sordid, heart-wrenching triangle. Grace, likewise, fondly thought that Al's dark secret was probably connected with business or some such more palatable sin.

One morning, Lisa had been first to reach the gate as a letter arrived, against all odds as she was not an early riser. "Ah hah, what's this?" she bellowed, clutching a feminine envelope in her hand. She ripped it open and digested the contents before Al had time to react.

The secret of Al's time in Taiwan was not only out. It was shouting itself across the room. Grace's relationship with her newfound love had been a secret across the waters, too. It was kept from her friends and family as they would surely have disapproved of such a connection with a Westerner and one so much more senior than she was at that time. Nevertheless, her family had finally discovered the truth, and she had been ostracized inside her own home. Now, Lisa and everybody in Al's life knew about it. In some ways, it was a relief. The pretense and subterfuge had been telling on him. Despite this relief, he had very little time to explain his miserable existence to the girl across the sea. If he didn't, surely Lisa would inform her on his behalf and that would destroy everything. It probably had no chance anyway, but he was desperate to try. Although it was the hardest letter he had to write, he finally accomplished it.

The reply was addressed to Lisa, not to him. "I'm out of Mr. Al's game, and I hope you will be happy," it continued. Lisa couldn't contain some trace of a smile of vengeful satisfaction. Phone calls did no good. Grace wouldn't talk to Al or would just cry into the receiver. The odd man's world began to crumble. His second marriage, such as it was, was effectively over. Now, when he needed her most, Hilary, too, seemed to fail him. The magic was still between them, but she offered little comfort. Perhaps she thought it served him right.

Mr. Roberts' four-week visit back to America to answer further charges in the courts brought by the opportunistic Rachael didn't help matters either. The strange thoughts began to get louder again. He had lost his children, his home, most of his remaining money, and now his precious China girl who had seemingly willed him out of her heart.

Al returned to the Philippines in a basic preparation for his death. The bottle would surely hasten that along. Hilary was still there, although Lisa and Princess had gone. A broken heart was bad enough, but one that had been cracked in numerous places was more than any man could bear. Hilary was all he had, but he had wanted her for so long. "Will you be mine now?" he asked repeatedly, but again, the answers of his typist lover were hesitating and evasive. "Perhaps in time, if Grace is really gone," she mumbled in between the giving of a coy kiss. Confusion was paramount in Al's mind as he could not be happy about the loss of that unusual girl who had chanced into his life. Neither could he be happy if Hilary packed her bags for good or if their lover's game continued with no resolution.

One morning, the remains of what had been a dynamic Mr. Roberts, traveler, and artist, reached across his bottle to answer the phone. His heart choked within him to hear Grace's voice. She hated him but still loved him and would fly to see him no matter what. Her family's bitter opposition could not dissuade her. Al didn't know what to do or where to turn. He had to be reunited with his China girl, but how could he stand a final parting of ways with the lovely secretary who had shared so many of his days and nights and whose body chemistry could still haunt him? The buzzing in his head became louder and louder, but there was no choice. The only destiny that could possibly save him and make him happy was unfolding and had him fast in its grip. Only actions can ultimately be the test of love, which is real and meant to be. Expressions of feeling and dreams could never drive out the inner voices of the dark side of Al's soul.

Hilary packed and left. He was sad and felt that bitter frustration that years of a doomed love leave in their wake. Yet the internal chorus began to quieten. Al could feel the sunshine and hear the birds sing at last. The shadow of a way out of a confused life was beginning to appear. Six months later, he and Grace got married on a sunny afternoon. In time, even her family accepted him into their own and he could sometimes hope. The bitterness between him and Lisa had quickly been forgotten, but he was able to see his beloved daughter again.

Still the strangeness persisted, and the inner melody of a discordant tune would occasionally perform for Al. He didn't understand why. His business would not succeed no matter how hard he tried and every dealing he had with bureaucracies and the normal instrumentalities of life was a sour battle. The court battles with Rachael had long ago been resolved, to his loss not so surprisingly, but he and Grace couldn't get an even break. One problem would surface after another. His parents had allowed Rachael over the years to influence them through Al's son, over whom so many battles had been fought. Al had been replaced completely as an influence on the child's life. The grandparents had become the parents, and Al had been consigned to the ranks of "the family loser," whom nobody took seriously. "I try to do my best, Dad," effused the ever so subtle Rachael on the phone one day, "But it's so hard to bring up a child on my own, and that useless Al doesn't help." Al and his China girl looked sad but could say or do nothing. In his parents' eyes, Al was a loser, and no warnings he could give them would be heeded. The bad luck just kept coming, and even a visit to Al's relatives now caused more dissension than pleasure. The sounds inside Al's mind began to increase their volume.

The cloud had always been there for this 'different' man. He had come almost to believe what the others believed. Somehow, there was a weakness or darkness inside him that would always prevent him from succeeding or being happy at anything. The lifting of the cloud was as sudden as it was unexpected. Rachael had been killed in a car crash while driving intoxicated on her way home from a disco.

At that moment, there was silence in Al's head. He smiled the smile of one who had been freed from a long and painful bondage. The love of a girl whose love he had no right to expect or deserve had inexplicably saved him from a malevolence that he likewise had not deserved. Sometimes, love is stronger than fate and can subsume it. Al's children and all the people he loved in time found fruitful and happy lives. Al Roberts always remembered the words of the priest who had married Grace and him. "Faith, hope, and love, but of these, the greatest is love." The good book's words had become deeds in Al's life before he had ever heard them. Life had come full circle.

The End

©John R. Spencer 1994

The Antique Typewriter

It was a goddam awful life. He wasn't quite sure if he had been forced into it by lack of opportunity or if some willful, perverse streak in his nature had brought him to this point. Yet here he was, up to the eyeballs in debt and in the constant presence of a harpy who passed as his wife. Each day was an endless agony, each tomorrow another possibility for disillusionment. However, life at the bottom presents few choices, so there wasn't a whole lot of thinking to do between beers.

The locals called him 'Frank'; nobody remembered why or what his real name was. The drunk from the pub who claimed to be a writer; that's all he was. He was able to earn just enough money to have an excuse for avoiding real work. The harpy, his wife, said that, and she, of all people, should know. 'Frank' had hit the relative big time, a travel piece on the delights of Melbourne in winter. He'd only spent a hundred dollars at the pub on its strength when disaster struck.

Barely half a line into the piece, his Japanese-made computer decided to pack up. "A loose wire can cost a fortune in this business," the repair man had remarked. Frank simply didn't have the money. A philosophical nature, a thousand nags from the harpy, and many constitutional schooners saw Frank a little closer to despair than usual.

Last night at the pub had been no different from usual. The blonde with the big tits had told him to F... off, and the guys kept insisting it was his shout. At closing time, he didn't have the money for a cab, and he was forced to accept a modicum of exercise in order to get home. Lurching from doorway to doorway, he passed the second-hand shop whose window he had so often urinated on before. There in front of him was a decrepit, ancient typewriter with a "$20" sign on it.

"A deadline is a deadline, after all," mused Frank. The next day, he sheepishly carried home the pile of junk while the harpy was out. Into the text of his story about winter in the southern capital he inserted the words, "Tullamarine airport was closed for the first time ever due to heavy snow on the runway." "Poetic license is always good for a few bucks," smiled Frank.

Over his third beer of the afternoon, while the harpy was out shopping, Frank was vaguely listening to the radio. "News flash," echoed the voice. "All flights to Tullamarine have been diverted to Sydney until further notice due to freak snowstorms."

Frank chuckled that wry gurgle of those who never seem to get an even break. "Ironic, but it wasn't going to help him. The harpy would see to that." Frank of a Thousand Pubs also wrote fiction stories; not that he ever sold any. At least it was something to do in between beers and wet daydreams about countless naked, succulent women knocking on his door.

"The dragon, otherwise called Arthur's wife, was hit by a gravel truck as she left a "No Sex" meeting. However, it wasn't the police who knocked on his door. A busty young girl whose ashen blonde hair licked at her upper assets stood naked before him when he answered the knock. 'Arthur, I was sent to soften the blow in a way that only you and God could understand.' Arthur's joy exploded almost before the girl could reach his arms."

Frank had just finished sipping a beer and typing the words on his temporary equipment when the doorbell sounded. A large, fat, and obviously male policeman stood before him. "I'm afraid I have some bad news for you, sir," he droned. "Your lady wife was hit by a drunk driver as she left a bingo meeting. She's dead." Frank's expression was nothing. He just stood there and thanked the constable for breaking the terrible news. One and a half seconds after he had closed the door, he let go a belly laugh that must have awakened the dead.

Frank was just opening his tenth beer of the day when there was another knock at the door. He was enjoying his newfound freedom and peace and resented the disturbance. "What the Fuck, do you want?" he screamed as he got up. Through the locked door came a silken reply. "Special pizza for you, sir." Frank was halfway through explaining that he didn't order a pizza when he opened the door.

His beer crashed to the floor anonymously; his cigarette burned his lip on its way down. In front of him was not only a more than adequate pizza but the most beautiful girl he had ever seen, stark naked. Her long black hair flowed over her proud, erect nipples, stopping just above her belly button and magic triangle. The naked girl invited herself in, the cheeks of her backside laughing at those outside who may have been fortunate enough to catch a glimpse.

The nowhere man couldn't believe it. Sex and attention that he had never even dreamed of, at least not since the harpy had got him. Tits and bum and succulent flower taunted him until he was exhausted. All he could mouth was one word, "unbelievable." He tried to get up, but the magic body of the girl would pin him down and beg for more.

"You can get me back anytime you want," were her parting words. Frank was much quieter than usual down the pub the next day. He didn't say much because he didn't know what to say. Strange thoughts echoed in his head. He didn't know what to make of it. His friends gave him their condolences about his wife and unsuccessfully tried to hide their smiles.

His next story was about a guy whose best friend had bought him a lotto ticket, which, strangely enough, had won. "I'll be lucky to sell this rubbish," mused Frank over his second beer of the day. The phone kept ringing, so he was forced to answer it. "Congratulations, sir, you have won eight hundred thousand dollars." "Don't come the raw prawn with me, mate!" Frank's response was quick and decisive. "I don't buy tickets, so I can't be a winner, can I?" "But sir, Mr. D.B. Somerton has named you as the beneficiary of the winning coupon."

It's always hard to argue with good news, and so it was when Frank replaced the receiver. "Yachts, girls, champagne;" it was all too much for him. Then he saw the typewriter. The rusting piece of junk was a fill-in until his computer could be repaired. Frank stared at it, but it didn't move or perform any tricks.

"This is the three genies and four wishes trick, or is it the other way around?" thought Frank. For a change, he was sober today. The muse buzzed loudly in his head, "Better get to work, Frank. The pubs are nearly closed, and you may be rich, but you're still not happy." The newly-freed-from-bondage writer drank a large swallow of "Uncle Jack" (he could afford it now) and sat down.

Frank thought carefully as his fingers reached the keys. He was no rich simpleton. He had struggled too hard for too long. No turd fairy third wish would destroy this boy! Money, he had it. Chicks, they were there for the asking, including the goddess with the black hair who had roused him from his life. He sat still for an hour, watching the street boys destroy some public property from his window. Then, deliberately, his fingers moved along the keys like a drunk man trying to fool the world.

He smiled the smile of the gods, the smile of one who knows and has been there. Letter by letter, the ancient machine made its mark on the page. "John (the story's hero) had reached his nemesis and surpassed it. Not only was he happy, but he also had no more problems."

As Frank stood up to get a beer, a crippling pain struck at his midriff. He bent double; he couldn't breathe, and his eyes rolled. He hit the ground hard. He had no more problems!

The End

© John Spencer 1994

The Black Bag

It was an old hotel in the back blocks of London's West End. It had been closed for ten years, just standing there decaying slowly, a little like the prestige of the monarchy. Another piece of the past headed for an inglorious future. "Edward's Palace of Rest" simply stood its ground, neither competing with the new nor graciously stepping aside for it.

Terry couldn't understand why he had to waste a day of his life listening to some old fart telling him how they dismantled rusting pipes in the 1920s. A bright youngster in his final year of mechanical engineering at one of the reasonable, if not renowned, universities, Terry didn't believe in wasting time. From the pinnacles of government down to the ancient institutions of learning, the British orthodoxy is renowned for periodically institutionalizing some strange and pointless idea. There it was. Every student had to spend one day receiving instruction in an unknown and totally unrelated field. The luckless lad had been assigned to learn plumbing demolition at "Edward's Palace of Rest." The crumbling exterior facade of pseudo-Edwardian architecture merely promised worse within.

That "worse" soon introduced itself in the form of Horace the Hose, Terry's mentor and supervisor for the day. Horace was a

crusty old relic of nineteenth-century British plumbing, appropriately specializing in the dismantling and destruction of ironwork, which he must have grown up with. However, Horace was much more famed for his habit of pissing when and where he felt like it than he was for his plumbing prowess.

"Get your butt over here, son," Horace boomed on Terry's arrival. "Give me a hand with these 'ere pipes." Sidestepping a foul-smelling puddle on the floor, the young man could see his "boss for the day" taking on some copper pipes protruding from the bottom of an ancient, enameled bathtub and losing. Horace loved to shout. "You take this 'ere wrench and screw those plate mounts loose. Then you take this 'ere hammer, and you knock the whole kit and kaboodle down. Think you can manage that, boy? I've got to go down to the pub for an hour to see some lads about a debt."

Horace left his young victim staring at inches of mold and black grime that must have had hundreds of dirty stories to tell, sordid tales of baths communal and other unimaginable filth. Thirty minutes of youthful strength and a good use of a wrench that hadn't been made in Taiwan saw the plate mounts kicked back to the Stone Age. Three blows of the hammer saw the entire bath break in two and ungraciously move in its death throws.

There, sticking out of the scum where the tub had been, was the tip of a black medical bag, such as Jack the Ripper supposedly used to such good effect. The young student carefully retrieved it and, with a touch of youthful vandalism, smashed the lock. Terry expected to see some old medical instruments, bloodstained or not, inside the decrepit leather enclosure. He was simply not prepared for what lay there.

Bundles on bundles of the old style five pound notes, the white ones which look like works of art. There must have been several thousand pounds in all. Next to this lovely pile of antique paper lay four large sheets of old-style, unperforated postage stamps. The engineering student could only stare, his mouth open.

"What you got there, boy?" Horace the Hose had returned from the pub, all primed for another afternoon's careless slashing. The crusty relic of the British empire grabbed the object from the lad's hand and peered within. "Gawd Almighty, stone the crows." Terry was smiling. "I reckon half each is the go," dared the student. "After all, this building's been unused for more than ten years. The stuff can't actually belong to anybody, can it?"

Horace looked at the young man, his upper lip twitching. "That's dishonest, boy. Nothing good ever comes from dishonesty. If we'd all thought like that, we'd never have 'ad an effin empire, would we? I'll take it to the police station right now. If the rightful owner claims it within six months, we've done the right thing. If he or she doesn't claim it, then it's ours as the finders. "but, but.....Sir," muttered Terry. "no buts, boy, it's done." Horace disappeared. Terry went home with something of an early mark as his assignment was completed.

Two months later, the young engineering student graduated and found a job in the west country. A couple of weeks after that, Terry, by chance, had run into a mutual acquaintance of himself and Horace the Hose. "What's the old fart doing?" the student inquired. "Still insulting people and crapping on about the empire?"

"No way, mate. It seems he came into an awful lot of money, won a lottery or something. He dumped his missus and his kids and moved to Teneriffe in the Canary Islands. Apparently, he's living in some mansion with some model who was recently Miss Sweden." "I suppose he's really happy and not miserable at all?" Terry innocently asked. "Too bloody right, mate. What's the effin' British empire and a few old pipes compared to life in Teneriffe with Miss Sweden?"

The End

© John Spencer 1994

The Prize

"Can't you find anything better to do?" snapped Sally, her head poking around the kitchen door. "There's plenty of washing up, and there's always the vacuuming, you know!"

"I'm nearly finished," replied Robert as he entered another word on the grid. "Don't you want us to win a grand?" he added, kicking the pile of magazines on the floor.

At that moment, a crash echoed through the kitchen, followed by an expletive from Sally. Eight giant packets of Cornflakes had found their way from a precarious perch onto the floor, their glossy labels mocking the woman's irate gaze. "Win two weeks in Paradise indeed," she snarled. "Who'd want two weeks in Southern Cambodia anyway?"

"I'm a firm believer in the law of averages," crooned Robert as he took a break from chewing his pen. "We're due to win something big any day now, and the fact that a lot of chicken shits are scared of the Khmer Rouge and won't enter will only increase our chances. And since we haven't had a holiday in three years, I'd have thought that you, of all people, would encourage me!"

"Aghgah!" The shrill response from amongst the pile of displaced cardboard seemed closer to despair than usual. "We would have had enough money for a week in the snow by now if you hadn't bought all that junk and wasted all that money on stamps!"

Robert stayed silent. He knew it was impossible to remain unlucky forever. His hour would come. "Besides," he pondered, "I've got to do something to keep interested in life." His job at the factory barely brought in a subsistence wage and was hardly intellectually stimulating. Sally and he had been married for six years, and their relationship had degenerated into one of a smoldering, repressed standoff. They hadn't produced any children, which didn't surprise Robert. Sally was always too tired from yelling at him to be interested in much of a sex life. Not that they could financially afford children anyway.

Sally, at 26, was a tall and attractive, leggy blonde with suggestive thighs. She emerged from the kitchen and plonked herself in front of the television as a romance movie was about to begin. "You can't watch that channel!" screeched her husband. "At 8.30, it's time for Feral Vacations, and tonight, they're giving away a one-week trip for two to Alice Springs. I reckon if we ring up the 0055 number at least ten times, we'd have a good chance."

"I'll feral you in a minute," retorted Sally as she guarded the TV, knowing she had just saved at least five dollars from their next phone bill.

The next day, on his way home from work, Robert stopped at the supermarket to pick up some milk. As he passed the health aid stand, he couldn't help but notice the special offer being made by "Eazy Clean" mouthwash. "$1 cashback off normal purchase price AND a chance to win a brand-new Commodore."

"6 x ($5.84 - $1) = $29.04," he calculated as he added half a dozen bottles to his trolley. It was true that he was forty dollars short in the rent money this week, and Mrs. Gibbens, the landlady, was not the most patient of souls. But God knows they needed a car and could never afford to buy one. "Besides," Robert justified to himself, "There's a good chance some money will come in the mail before Friday."

When he arrived home, he was careful to put the mouthwash away before Sally returned from her real estate class.

"By the way," said Sally as she was laying the table for the evening meal, "I saw Brenda Stanford on the bus today. We really must invite her and David for a dinner party soon. We've eaten at their place eight times, and they haven't been over here once."

"You're right," replied Robert, "But it'll have to wait a while. We can't afford the extra expense of fancy meals just yet."

"Wait! How long? We're getting a reputation for being cheap Charlies. If we don't return some of the invitations and favors we owe, we won't have any friends left!"

"Very soon, some of our investments are bound to pay off, and we'll have plenty of spare cash. Then we can look after our friends, get a car, and go on a holiday to Europe," soothed her husband. "Besides," he said to himself, "someone has to win the two competitions and the Pools each week. It could be my turn any time."

It was true that at thirty years of age, Robert wasn't exactly at the pinnacle of success, economic or any other kind. He and Sally had no significant assets, no house, no car, and no money in the bank. They were barely keeping their heads above water in an endless whirlpool of debt, bills and crippling expenses. However, Robert was just biding his time, or to put it more accurately, having his time bided for him. As a man of great vision, he had spent years laying the groundwork for his number to come up. He would enter the new phase of the winning streak any day now. Statistically speaking, it was time.

When XXX magazine announced its latest contest and offered a night with Divine Brown as the winner's reward, the latent genius and soon-to-be-rich factory hand dutifully entered. True, there was no huge stash of cash to be won, but statistics demanded that he enter as many competitions as possible, both great and small, and there was something deliciously wicked about this particular prospect. Robert couldn't remember the last time he had experienced an all-in, wet and wild, passionate bit of nooky with no holds barred, and the mere thought caused a sudden stirring in his trousers.

"A divine night with Brown - black - pink bits - brown," the envisaged debauchery fired his imagination. "Black forest shielding tender pink young growler... Mmmmm." The task at hand wasn't too difficult. Twenty-five words about what he and Miss Brown could do without a car and why he thought he should be chosen. After neatly clipping the appropriate coupon, he chucked the magazine onto the loungeroom floor, where it competed for space with "Your Home My Castle," "Hot Teen," and numerous other titles.

The following month was much the same as the last: fourteen crosswords, seventeen lucky draws, thirty-five 0055 calls, and two contests of "skill" with sleep and hours at the factory in between. None of Robert's friends called by, and Sally's girlfriends loathed him at the best of times. Rita and Marge, in particular, had been encouraging her to seek a divorce, but she hadn't got around to it. "Mind you," Marge had chuckled once, "he hasn't got anything to divorce him for!"

When Robert opened his mail one Tuesday evening, he wasn't quite prepared for what lay in store. The third envelope, with its fancy, squirrely printing, took him by surprise. Despite his unwavering conviction in his own destiny, he found it hard to believe its contents.

"Congratulations, Mr. Robert Adams, you are the lucky winner of our "Night with Divine Brown" contest. Miss Brown will be waiting for you at the Hilton in your capital city of residence - i.e., Melbourne. Please present yourself at the presidential suite at 7 pm on the evening of September 2. Good luck, and enjoy your prize."

When his good (and much-deserved) fortune had finally sunk in, Robert was all smiles. Half an hour later, when Sally entered, he kissed her on the cheek. "You look tired. Let me cook dinner tonight." Sally appeared perplexed. "You sick or something, Rob?" Still, such opportunities didn't come very often, so she made the most of it.

For the next couple of weeks, her other half was unbearably nice. He had even taken to doing his crosswords in the toilet where she wouldn't have to be an unwilling witness. One breakfast time, as he was washing the plates, Robert caught Sally's attention. "I'm sorry dear, but I have to go to a training course in Brisbane next week. The factory is considering making me a foreman. I'll be away on Saturday night and possibly Sunday as well, depending on the flights."

"At last, you seem to be showing some sense," affirmed his leggy partner. "I've always said you've got to work for things. You're never going to win anything worthwhile, you know." Robert just smiled.

The following Saturday morning, he left the house in a taxi in the direction of the airport. "Thanks, buddy," he mumbled as he alighted from the cab somewhere along the length of Flinders Street. The remaining hours were idled away with a tasty cafe lunch, a couple of bets on the TAB, and a few constitutional ales.

Five o'clock came and went, followed by six. At 6:30, he bade farewell to a mystified barman with a "See ya. Black is beautiful, bro." Arriving by tram at the Hilton on the Park, Robert presented himself at the reception. Not only was he expected, he was given the full VIP treatment. "Have a drink in the bar, Sir, and everything will be ready. It's on the house."

A short time later, a bell boy and two bell girls showed the fortunate man to his rendezvous with destiny in the presidential suite. They opened the door for him and wished him a good night. Robert strolled in with the gait of a cock of the walk. He knew where his exotic promise would be waiting and strode past the lounge to the bedroom.

A dark and curvaceous figure was largely obscured by the bedclothes. "I see ya, honey," he called, trying to sound like Bogart. Smiling, he snatched back the sheets, baring the figure beneath.

A black and busty blow-up doll stared blankly up at him, its orifices looking pathetically still. Just above the plastic and nylon fanny was scrawled the word "loser." Before his jaw had time to drop, a dozen laughing and jeering women burst from hiding.

"Surprise!" cackled Rita, with Marge and Sally standing just behind her. He was the grand finale of their hen's party.

The End

© John Spencer 1995

Lesbian Lay Gone Wrong

It was at one of those fantastic, everything goes parties that only the gay community can seem to successfully put on. While 90% of the blokes were gay, and half of the chicks there were straight, so if you could pass the obstacles unscathed, you were in with a good chance. This hedonistic event had begun at noon and drifted down to the tidal swimming pool at the back of the house.

I noticed a tall, well-endowed brunette in her twenties. It was hard not to notice her. She emerged from the pool, her clinging, wet T-shirt accentuating her shapely, full breasts and her soaking wet, white cotton panties outlining the V mound of a succulent crotch. Tufts of black foliage peeped out from the edges, making a challenging visual tease. Annie was a hard-core lesbian, so I was informed. However, she obviously liked me and seemed to be in the mood to try something different. The party raged, and with the copious refreshments available, we were both nicely oiled. As the sun disappeared in the west, the crowd moved up the hill back to the house. Annie and I, sensing each other's inclination, strayed and, losing ourselves in the garden, found a hospitable-looking bush. Peeled off its T-shirt and panties, her body looked and smelled better than ever. Her hot, fur-covered snatch was moist, ready for action, and demanding. We had been missed. In the distance, people were searching for us, calling our names.

At that moment, disaster struck. My John Thomas decided that it was a water snake and didn't appreciate the oiling my system had enjoyed. The wretched thing went on strike, then and there, with one of the worst cases of brewer's droop imaginable. Nothing would work. The unimpressed brunette returned to the party, followed by myself and the traitor between my legs.

Annie must have talked somewhat as, when I entered the crowded room, a dozen laughing voices yelled, "Welcome back, half-mast!" and Annie mumbled something about sticking to women in the future.

The End

(c) John Spencer 1994

The Society Man

It was a crisp and clear Canberra morning. At the age of 47, Phil Hartley had been employed in the Public Service for twenty-four years and had reached the lower level of the middle echelons in his quest for success. "Come in here for a minute, please, Phil," his boss crooned from his office. "With all the cutbacks in the department, it'll probably be no surprise to learn that we are reducing staffing levels." The junior bureaucrat mumbled assent as the boss continued. "You've got the bullet, I'm afraid, and your retrenchment package commences at the end of the month.

Phil Hartley was devastated. Much as he hated his boring job, at least it was a job. Now, he would have nothing to do and little money to do it with. There was no golden handshake. In these austere times, the handshake was more of the dusty broom variety. Phil had served the wheels of government bureaucracy for all that time, and for what? There was no recognition

or thanks, no accumulated wealth, and he'd really only made the country he lived in worse when all was said and done.

Emily Hartley didn't waste much time before heading

off to a new life in the black BMW of an upwardly mobile used car salesman. Ten years Phil's junior, at least she had a future. Their daughter, Vanessa, was

grown up and in the Navy. Brad, his BMW, and Emily would be going places and fast while Phil sat in front of the telly mumbling over and over, "What the fuck am I going to do?" With all this sudden spare time on his hands, Phil thought he should make a useful contribution to society and find something worthwhile to keep himself busy.

As he picked up a greasy strip of bacon from the newspaper one morning, Phil could hardly fail to notice the headlines. "Anarchist terror strikes! The third politician meets a violent death." Underneath was the gruesome account of how the transport minister had been hacked to death by an unknown assailant as he was leaving an upmarket establishment in a prominent red-light area. The week before, the health minister had been the victim of a clumsy murder staged to look like a suicide, and the week before that, a state education minister had been deliberately run over in a Perth car park.

Superintendent Adam McIntosh and Detective Inspector David Gleeson of the special task force pored over their notes at headquarters. "This is a bastard of a case," mumbled the superintendent, otherwise known as the Big Mac, because of his generous proportions. "With that first case in WA, I thought it was going to be simple. Angry parents or some disgruntled thug of a high school student.

"Anything involving politicians is never simple; it's only the electorate that's simple," chortled Gleeson. "That poor transport bloke getting laid, the chop and laid out all in

succession," he continued, "And then the killing of the health minister with a syringe full of concentrated

nicotine. I've never seen

anything like it." At that moment, the pair were interrupted by a junior sergeant.

"Excuse me, Sir, they've just found another one. Here is the report." The sergeant disappeared. The Big Mac cursed. "Shit! The Minister for Foreign Affairs has taken his final trip.

Cyanide gas in a canister fired into his bedroom from a

grenade launcher."

"What do you make of all this Mac?" Gleeson asked

nervously. "I'm stumped, and the country's in an uproar. We've got to do something."

The big man eased back in his chair as he let off a humungous fart which caused his colleague to duck.

"There has got to be a common link. The victims come from all sides of politics at all levels." "If we don't solve this and quick," Gleeson interrupted,

"They' 11 all be asking for danger money on top of their other allowances." The entire building was abuzz with tension and excitement, the buzz of an engine revolving at high speed but going nowhere.

In between his stints on Lifeline and lending a helping hand to the Smith Family and Vinnies, Phil Hartley had been taking it easy with the odd short fishing holiday to ponder his future. He baited his hook and cast into the breakers of Avoca Beach on the NSW Central Coast. "I can't afford to keep paying the rent," he ruminated, "But I'm not eligible for any government assistance. At my age, no one's going to give me another job." He was awakened from his reverie by a flash of pink and gold. A young blonde who had been nude sunbathing behind a saltbush had just stood up. The useless stirring in his loins reminded Phil how few personal options lay before him.

Directing his attention back to the line and the sea, he went on playing with his thoughts. "If only they would put him on the list for government-subsidized housing. Still, lots of people were worse off than him. The big boss had said that before leaving Phil's farewell party in his Mercedes.

In an Adelaide newspaper office, a journalist held up a grubby piece of paper with a message scrawled in cut-out letters. "What do you make of this?" he asked expectantly of his editor. The editor adjusted her glasses and stared at the three short lines. "Recycling begins at home. Affirmative action is necessary for a friendly environment. The meaning of life is a broom." The editor scoffed. "Just another psycho crank. Chuck it in the bin."

A prominent Melbourne newspaper took more care of the note they received in the mail and ran an afternoon headline of "Female Jack the Ripper stalks officials!" The typed message had simply said, "I'm not a disgruntled cop Nor a fresh-faced nipper; I'm just a fun-loving lass.

Yours affectionately,

Sexy Sandra, the little ripper."

And so life went on. The government was even more confused than usual, and for the first time, its members had a rough idea of what it felt like to be the victim of someone else's program. Despite massive security, the Deputy Leader of the Opposition, two government MPs, and a junior diplomat had been poisoned at a cocktail party by French champagne laced with brucine.

"Strewth!" exclaimed the Big Mac to Gleeson and the rest of the team." A government ethnic affairs spokesman has been gunned down as he left a meeting. I thought at least they were a protected species." Some serious thinking settled over the room, and the computers were kept busy. "This bitch is just so careful," remarked one of the junior members of the task force. "No useful leads at any of the crime

scenes whatsoever. She must have the natural habit of

never identifying herself in whatever she does!"

"Now, now!" interjected McIntosh. "You can't believe everything you read in the papers you know. We're not certain that it is a woman. In fact, we're not certain of much at all."

Another week rolled by and Phil was watching the cricket on the telly. He enjoyed a game where the result was apparently not certain beforehand. The heavy knock on the door caused him to start.

He was pushed to the ground and handcuffed by two burly constables as the swat team, rifles leveled, looked on in the background. "Are you Mr. Philip Hartley?" a deep voice boomed. When Phil replied in the affirmative, the voice droned on, "You have the right to remain silent; you have the right to…."

Back at the station, Phil quickly confessed. "How did you know?" he inquired during the interrogation. "It was pretty simple, really," answered Gleeson. We just searched all our computer records for people who were heavily involved in charity work at the same time as they were financially strapped. We took an especially hard look at ex-government employees. You fitted the psychological profile perfectly."

The attempt in Parliament to suddenly introduce the death penalty had failed, and Phil Hartley found himself with free government housing for life. As he settled into Grafton gaol, things on the outside were getting back to normal. The new Foreign Affairs minister, on a visit to China, had just taken his first bribe from the portfolio.

The End

(C) John Spencer 1996

Marilyn At Midnight

Marilyn looked marvelous, her well-endowed upper portions tantalizingly balanced by those renowned thighs and the impishly cheeky view of her parting angle. The golden locks men would die for fluttered gently in the breeze whilst her ashen skirt eddied around those seductive legs.

Brad thanked a windy day for making his glimpse of perfection complete. After all, it's not often, even in one's dreams, that one gets a treat like that, let alone in real life. If there were a single spot in the universe that he wanted to be, he'd spotted his if, albeit a triangular version thereof. "Lust, lust, lust; you can have everything else, and I'll be happy with that I trust." Life, love, and the cause instantly took second place, and somehow it seemed natural.

Bang, bang, splut, splut, tat tat!. The shots were all over the place. "Whoever was responsible was more likely to hit their mother than what they were aiming at," thought Brad momentarily as he dived behind a garbage bin. The heavy but not unwelcome shape on top of him flashed a promise of pink and blonde as well as further protection.

"Ooh! That's nasty," sighed Marilyn as she disentangled herself from the gasping body beneath. "Fuck! Isn't it?" mumbled the body in question. Against the anarchic background of further staccato noise, the meeting took shape. "What's a nice girl like you doing in a place like this?" Brad stammered before he could help himself. "I'm working," cooed the soft and sensual voice. "What about you?" Brad rose to his knees. "Worked in fucking guns all me life, and now they want me to starve! Is the gun buyback going to give me a golden handshake and a pension for life?" Before I go out the back door, I thought I'd make me presence felt by way of protest."

The futile protest against further government controls on life was wasted against the wrath of the elements and the random cyclone of bullets. Whoever fired the shots and whoever cared, circumstances made a mockery of individual effort and heroism. As the wail of sirens announced the end of the day's proceedings, an unemployed gunsmith and his blonde vision from the past limped from the scene together. "What's your name anyway?" stuttered a rather confused Brad. "Why Norma, Norma Jean," purred the silky voice. "Perhaps you and me need a little drinky, winky back at my hotel."

It was like something out of those fifties James Dean type movies. This sort of luck just did not occur in the nineties. Back at the "2000" hotel, Brad was still bemused. "Norma, you know why I was there, but what the heck do you want with me, and why were you wasting your time in small town Australia?" She smiled like a Venus on heat and kissed him softly on the fly. "Since you asked Honeychile, and I'm getting nowhere with this assignment, I'll tell you the truth. "My!' ol' Uncle Sam sent me here to learn what is going on with our! 'ol' below-the-belt neighbor and ally. Who runs your country, the collective states or that abandoned rabbit warren known as Canberra? From what we hear back home, that mob hibernates every time the prostitutes move out of town!"

Brad felt the zip on his fly commit suicide as he gazed at those opposing thighs with their inbuilt challenge. "Come on, Aussie, come on!" was ringing in his ears as the blue eyes and their pink counterparts questioned him. "If you like me, you could give me all the names of the pro-gun lobby and their opposite numbers, and if you were a real sweetie, you might tell me which politicians support state rights and which ones are still recovering from the last time the call girls surrendered the city of flies to their bureaucratic counterparts.

A voice whispered in the young man's ear. "Do the right thing! Listen to the important voices." Instantaneously, Brad spilled everything he knew as Marilyn, I mean Norma, unbuttoned her blouse due to the heat. The mere nakedness of her bosoms with their pink love finders was unbearable. "I'll tell you anything!" screamed the unemployed gunsmith. "I love you! I've always loved you! Please!"

There was no audible voice. Only the sound of an ashen dress effortlessly hitting the floor. As the pure white panties followed suit and Brad was faced with a golden bush laughing at him, the torture was pure ecstasy. No one on Earth could resist the smile of those pinkish wiggly bits luring with the promise of their inner being. And so it was with our unemployed youth. The starlet was everything she had ever promised to be, from the outside heavenly apparition to the quintessential love juices of her inner core. Brad had seen such goddesses involved with countless other guys in so many movies, but now he had one to himself.

Just as he rolled over with that smile of one who had been there, a heavy knock on the door interrupted his dreams. "Federal Police! Open up! Now!" The naked youth reeled back from the widely flung door. "What's that in the bed then?" Detective Sergeant Mike Cawfield observed as he interviewed Marilyn (Norma). Senior Constable Brendan Fox placed a sturdy boot on the now prone torso of Brad just to make sure of the situation. "Clark," called Marilyn from the bed, "I never thought I'd see you again. What are you doing here?"

"Shut up! And come with us," yelled his sidekick, who looked suspiciously like Don Johnson (Whatever happened to Miami Vice anyway?) "Clark, I mean inspector Cawfield, can't help you now!" yelled the Don Johnson lookalike (Brendan Fox). "We know you're a front for the 'Shoot-up Australia movement. The fuckin' Yank accent just proves the point." At that, the duo bundled Marilyn naked and, in all her glory, to the adjoining room, which was fortuitously vacant.

The noises from the next room and the happy smell that wafted on the breeze told Brad that Marilyn knew exactly how to handle an interrogation. "Diplomacy begins in the... "Brad was getting really jealous, to say the least! He wasn't going to get lucky this once just to have it all taken away from him. But what could he do? They had guns! Fuming, ruminating, and wanking in the mind, Brad was still lying on the bed alone and impotent when Marilyn returned. "They've really lost their touch, you know!" They just couldn't take the pace and are still asleep. Let's go."

On the trans-Pacific flight, Marilyn explained to the young man with not much of a future that his knowledge of his country made him worth the ticket and then some, as she planted lipstick on his fear-bleached cheek, "Fuck the guns! Fuck violent movies, and fuck all the crap that they go on about! Whatever the outcome, the world will still be the same; criminals and maniacs will continue to shoot people on a needs basis. Nothing will change except millions of dollars will go to the bad people." "Yes then, but why...?"

"States rights! You schmuck," whispered Mariyln. The CIA is extremely interested in who or what holds the balance of power in Australia and anywhere else for that matter." The round of 'protected' parties and the high life from the West Coast to the East made Brad feel that he was worth something at last. At the presentation (of a big house in Beverley Hills and an income), Brad couldn't help but feel a little homesick as the PA blared the latest editions of "How Green is My Cactus!" But shit! Who would give it a further thought after moving into that mansion with the goddess that men would die for? As long as Brad could get it up he was in clover.

"What the fuck was Erroll Flynn doing in his bedroom?" As Marilyn disappeared on the shoulder of the intruder, Brad couldn't help but think he'd been set up. An unnamed ASIS agent being the culprit didn't make him feel any better. After all, he was an Australian (although his mother was a Kiwi), and people south of Hawaii had to earn their own good fortune-everyone knew that. After regaining consciousness from what must have been a star performance Brad sat looking at his socks. "Fuck this, he thought! They can have the fucking mansion; I just want my Marilyn (Norma) back!" After all, what's heaven if you can't get laid?"

Some spot of intrinsic genius crawled its way up from his dick to his brain, and Brad had an idea. "Erroll, Erroll, Erroll!" "No fucking hood is going to rob me of my glory," he mused while planning revenge. "The

Robin Hood Bar! Where else would an Errol Flynn lookalike hang out?" Since it wasn't that far off Sunset Boulevard, even Brad was able to find it. The fight was real Hollywood stuff- vicious but short-lived and without too much blood. Brad and Marilyn stepped over Erroll's body on their way to a better life.

Brad's only complaint about life with Marilyn in the mansion was that sometimes she lifted her legs when he was just plain too tired from the time before. Bliss! That had to be it! Just when Brad was about to do justice to the beckoning blonde-shrouded tunnel of the love goddess for the fourth time that day, a bright light shattered his intentions. It was like the day of Judgement, but it couldn't possibly be. As Marilyn fondled Brad's manhood and he quaked in fear, the words tripped out. "What's the black in the center of the brightness?" Marilyn smiled with a lost lover look. "It says, 'The End!"

"Marilyn is great! What a digitalization!" exclaimed Phil, the director. "'Downunder Love' is going to be a great CD movie! Jeremy, the computer effects producer, added, "Our dead stars' performances were superb all right, but who the hell is this Brad Nicholls guy? I've never heard of him! The movie is a goer, all right, but we have to edit it. Brad Nicholls out and replace him with Humphrey Bogart!"

The End

© John Spencer 1996

The Uniform

In early 1979, I visited a singles' bar on Sydney's North Shore. Such places are not, and were not then, the easiest of places to meet attractive and interested girls. The music, cider, and wine were pleasant, but the prospects of making an exciting liaison seldom increased from poor to mediocre. I had met a female friend at the bar and had been sitting chatting and listening to a guitar duo when I noticed a petite but gorgeous young lady at the next table. She was only about 5 ft 2 ins. Tall and possessed black, wavy hair and a smooth, pale skin. She personified my image of Snow White. She was alone and did not appear to be enjoying herself much. Ruth, my friend, engaged her in conversation, and she introduced herself as Helen. Her girlfriend had left earlier, and she hadn't felt up to driving home. At closing time, we all made our way down to the street. Ruth drove off, and I was preparing to do the same when Helen, with half a tear in her eyes, asked me if I could drive her home *as* she thought she had drunk a little too much to be able to safely take her car. I wasn't sure if she was interested in me or if she was simply telling the truth, but either way, I wasn't going to refuse the chance to know her better. Leaving my vehicle parked where it was, I drove hers to her house.

Helen was twenty-two years old and still lived with her parents in a large modern dwelling in an upmarket suburb. She invited me in for coffee, which I suppose was the least she could do since I needed to phone a cab back to my car. The pale skin of her hands responded to my touch, and her polished lips answered the caress of my mouth and tongue. The embrace became more passionate, and loosening her shirt and brassiere, my fingers gently fondled her not-too-large but firm and exquisitely shaped breasts. I could feel her nipples stiffen, and our kisses became deep and exploratory. From the moment I met Helen, I sensed that she was a somewhat reserved girl, so I took things slowly. Soon, the bulge in my trousers was raging, and her breath became shorter. Lightly running my hand under her skirt and along the insides of those silky thighs, I reached her cotton-clad pubic mound. Beneath that last obstacle, a thatch of curly, black hair and an already moist opening awaited. One of my wandering digits ever so gingerly teased her outer and inner lips and entered. The gateway to her love channel was narrow, and the interior, although well-lubricated, was very tight.

Without warning, Helen began to cry. She was obviously still a virgin and somewhat inhibited about expressing sexual desire. I apologized for upsetting her, made no further advances, and rang for a taxi. Over the next few weeks, I dated her regularly, but she would not allow my moves to go too far. I had begun to despair of ever possessing her, all the more so as her parents were overprotective and extremely suspicious. One night, I was taking Helen home after dinner, and had pulled up in her driveway when she turned and murmured, "Take me to your place. I want to sleep with you. "As I was reversing out of the drive, her tyrannical mother emerged from the house yelling, "Helen, come back!" We sped off into the dark.

Helen was a bank clerk, and as I had picked her up from work that evening, she was still wearing

her uniform, a white blouse, a short, and a blue skirt. I have always had a thing for girls in uniform, and there was more than a stirring in my loins long before we reached my apartment. She was taking the pill to regulate her periods, so her previous reluctance was not from fear of pregnancy. After a quick nightcap, I led her to my bed and, savoring every moment, began to remove her uniform. The blouse and the bra were my first prizes baring her succulent, firm tits. The blue skirt succumbed to the unfastening of button and zip and slid silently to the floor. Clad only in bikini briefs, her compact, lithe body fanned my carnal desire. She lay on the bed and waited as I discarded my own apparel. Removing her panties, I gazed upon her love box with its mat of curly, black hair. My tongue flickered over every inch of that region as I sipped her untried nectar. Her lower lips were even sweeter than those of her fair face, and as I explored every corner I could reach, her panting became rapid.

Climbing astride Helen, I inserted my rock-like organ into her entrance, taking care to hurt her as little as possible. As I pushed deeper, the head of my cock cast aside her hymen, and then my entire length was bathed with the sweetness of that unexplored canal. With each back-and-forth motion, I could feel her curly fur tickling the surface of my balls. The joy building up inside me was almost unbearable. The feel of her smooth, well-rounded bottom further intensified the sensation. When I came, my hot semen exploded and seemed to fill her entire passage. Although she hadn't peaked, she was close to it, and Helen's initiation into womanhood had caused her no great discomfort.

Despite her inexperience, I immediately began giving her lessons on taking my length in her mouth. The mere thought of her had me stiff as a pole in no time, and again, I entered her most intimate recess. Helen's love juices were flowing freely, and her cavity of joy was sliding along the length of my member with well-oiled ease. She lovingly teased my balls with her demure fingers each time I penetrated her. In turn, I tickled her asshole with my little finger. When my lady came, she kept coming. Her cries didn't cease until sometime after I had fired my bolt.

All the next day, we stayed in bed, making repeated love. Almost every imaginable position was covered in our lust. Helen couldn't stifle her ecstatic cries at all when I screwed her from behind, doggy style; as I drove deep into her, my playful teasing of her love button was more than she could bear. By the next evening, we could give no more, both exhausted and a little sore.

Throughout the weeks that followed, we saw and felt a lot of each other, and Helen's experience of pleasure-giving grew. However, the path to true passion, like the one to true love, never runs smoothly. The matriarch of her family was somewhat more puritanical than Queen Victoria, and on more than one occasion, my phone rang to be followed by vehement accusations against me as the corrupter of her daughter.

Damn it, her daughter was twenty-two, not thirteen, and she should be allowed to make her decisions in peace. Nevertheless, the voice would usually continue, "If you want to sleep with Helen, then you marry her!" I may have lost some sleep, but I didn't lose my desire for the girl.

Helen's nude body excited me to the extent that I wanted to possess every part of it. No orifice was safe; one day, after a particularly torrid bout of lovemaking, I could contain myself no more, and Helen was as hungry as myself. The cheeks of her backside and her tight, little anus looked inviting. As AIDS was a plague of the future at that time, no elaborate accessories were needed. We had been rubbing each other down with baby oil, and I asked Helen to liberally coat my straining appendage. I poured oil down the slit in her sensual buttocks and, embracing her from behind, began to explore that last passage of mystery. As my manhood penetrated that territory, her pleasure cries came thick and fast. Her beautiful body, so tightly interwoven with mine, was a feast of ecstasy. Before long, I climaxed, sending shudders through both our beings. Every time I saw Helen in her bank uniform, I had to take her to a private place fast. I'm sure her uniforms wore out in half the time that they took before.

© John Spencer 1991

The Millionaire's Daughter

At the end of 1976, I was twenty five and had just graduated with a teaching degree. While a student, I'd been driving taxis, and in two months, I would embark on a teaching career. I had heard fascinating tales of the East and decided to take a short vacation to Malaysia. On the flight to Kuala Lumper, I'd made the acquaintance of a group of other students and, by chance, ran into them a few days later in Ipoh, the country's third largest city and about a hundred miles north of the capital, I accompanied them to the market area as they were interested in shopping, Having little interest in buying souvenirs and the like I was standing alone on the sidewalk in front of a tailor's shop while my friends were busy inside. It was much more fascinating to soak up the balmy evening and watch the colorful throngs of people passing. After a few minutes, a tall, elegant Chinese girl with high cheekbones and long, flowing hair approached. She possessed fine features and looked every inch an Oriental princess. She was slender but perfectly in proportion. As the girl drew level she turned to me and winked, then kept walking.

I stood still, stunned for a couple of minutes, then realizing the folly of letting such a chance pass by, I set off in quick pursuit. It was nearly half a mile before I caught her disappearing into a haberdashery shop. I also entered and purchased some needles and thread for which I had no earthly use.

"What you need thread for?" inquired the girl. I quickly confessed to having followed her and introduced myself. Her name was Yoke Ching, but she called herself Sindy. She was eighteen years old and had finished school but had no job. Upon my invitation for coffee and supper, she replied, "Not time now. Meet me tomorrow behind the cinema on Ye Tak Street at 8 pm." The next day passed slowly for me, and by 8.25, I was still alone at the back of the theater. Then I heard a voice from the shadows. "John, over here." There was my princess looking as enchanting as ever but with a worried appearance. She explained that her father, a prominent and wealthy businessman, was looking for her, and she couldn't stay. Our rendezvous was set for the next night.

On this occasion, she was punctual and considerably more relaxed.

"Where would you like to go?" I asked, expecting a request for a movie or disco. "Your hotel," was her answer. My excitement grew as we walked the few blocks towards my temporary lodgings. Sindy walked a long way behind me and on the other side of the street as she couldn't afford to be seen in the company of a man, let alone a foreigner. We slipped up the hotel stairs as discreetly as possible until we were safe behind the locked door of my room with its softly whirring ceiling fan.

Her lithe body passionately embraced mine immediately. This princess is hungry for love; I mused to myself as her mouth and tongue explored mine with abandon. I helped her out of her high-fashion dress and plain brassiere. Her breasts were full and firm, with taut purple-pink nipples offsetting their smooth, sallow complexion. She removed my traveler's shirt and jeans with almost indecent haste and equally efficiently disposed of my underwear. Her regal fingers explored the entire area of my manhood with a light, although hungry, touch. As we fell onto the bed, Sindy pushed her body against me hard.

She was still wearing her panties, which were of the old-fashioned, full type and not the modern bikini variety. The shape and texture of her firm, rounded buttocks were as refined as the rest of her. Removing her last garment, I searched the sweet area between her well-formed thighs. A symmetrical triangle of fine, black hair was evenly distributed around the entrance to her inner sanctum. The purple labia of her exquisite fanny revealed a deeper pinkness, and as my lingering tongue caressed their enclosed love oyster, her pleasure groans were becoming too much for me. "I want you inside me now," Sindy breathed. She arched her back, extending her glistening and sensual crotch towards me. My bolt of muscle penetrated the purple lips and slid into that warm pinkness beyond. Sindy's inner heat drove me wild. With each stroke, the spasms of joy grew stronger. As I reached a shuddering climax, Sindy propelled herself backward off me, catching the head of my exposed shaft in her shapely mouth. She sucked each drop of cum carefully, savoring the moment.

To my disappointment, Sindy had to leave early and return home to avoid suspicion. We saw a lot of each other over the next few days and nights, but she would never walk with me in public. She introduced me to Jouanne, a close friend of hers. Jouanne was a year younger than Sindy and had a fuller figure. Her facial features were demonstrably Chinese, but her beauty was outstanding. The three of us spent a good deal of time together. I was scheduled to spend a week further north in Penang. Sindy promised to visit me there the next Saturday as she could then escape from her house for the day. Jouanne was free and wanted to come with me since Penang was a beach resort town.

Everything was arranged. Jouanne and I left on the bus, and Sindy would come the following Saturday. After the long, bumpy bus ride and a short ferry trip across Penang harbor, Jouanne and I checked into an old colonial-style hotel, which, with its central courtyard, was strongly reminiscent of the days of the British Raj. Upon entering the room, as the heat was enervating, I switched on the fan, removed my dusty clothes, and lay on the bed for an afternoon nap.

As Jouanne was Sindy's close friend, I wasn't expecting any romantic or sexual encounter. Nevertheless, I couldn't help observing her as she freshened up and stepped out of her dress. She stood, brushing her hair, the mirror behind her, clad only in a beige bra and bikini briefs. Her shapely form was fuller and slightly thicker set than her friend's. She discarded her bra and nonchalantly shook her shiny locks from side to side. Her proud breasts faced me unashamedly, and I felt my closest companion stiffen noticeably as I watched. By the time the girl threw herself on the bed to rest, my stirred blood had destroyed any ability to sleep. I lay there half watching her, and my rock-hard dick strained against my briefs. The perspiration on my brow was more from unslaked desire than the tropical humidity; overwhelming, but any unreciprocated move would result in severe embarrassment all round.

I half-heartedly leaned over Jouanne, and, smiling at her, I hungrily clicked my teeth. She reached up, pulled my lips to hers, and engaged me in a sudden, passionate kiss. She entwined her splendid body with mine, and her tongue searched in a frenzy. My mouth tasted her lips, her ears, and her bold nipples. Her ass was firm, had ample flesh, and felt very good to the touch. The V mound framed by the beige panties was pressing hard against me. I pulled her pants down those shapely thighs and discarded my own. Her pussy was compact and inviting. Its outer surface was smooth save for a dozen or so fine, downy hairs.

Her entrance was already humid to the touch, her vaginal muscles were strong, and the passage was very even and snug. With a few preliminaries, I eased the head of my now swollen cock inside and then inserted its entire length. For what seemed like an eternity, the tide of Jouanne's love juices flowed and ebbed, my manhood plundered deep into her succulent flesh and back again, and the well-endowed cheeks of her backside rose and fell in an ever-increasing rhythm. Our simultaneous orgasms were like a sexual catharsis. Exhausted, our soaking bodies finally submitted to the afternoon sleep. The week that followed saw a sweet reconnaissance of Jouanne's entire body. This talented girl and I got to know each other inside and out, so to speak. Our room in that old hotel provided an unusual backdrop for our lovemaking. Some malignant supernatural presence in the night on occasion had us both cringing in fear.

Saturday came, and along with it, my Asian princess, Sindy. The three of us, in the company of others, traveled to the palm-shaded Battafaringi beach for a picnic. Sindy was wearing the briefest of bikinis and, after a brief swim, demanded that I possess her immediately. She had indeed missed me. We strolled along the beach until we found a reasonably secluded spot behind some rocks. Impatiently, she took my full length in her mouth and seemed to devour it. When I had almost reached the point of no return, she withdrew, ripped off my trunks, and discarded her bikini bottom. Sindy's black triangle begged to be ravaged. I impelled my engorged rod hard into her waiting cavity, my fingers sinking into her exposed ass. My cock's penetration of her was total and rapid. By the time I deposited my load of jism into Sindy's inner recess, she was screaming like a banshee with euphoria; my princess had indeed arrived.

While on the return journey, I glanced from the bus window over the cliffs and down to the beach. The very spot of our tryst was in full view of the road! Towards the end of my vacation, I again had a chance encounter with the students from the plane. Their bags were bulging with souvenirs, while mine were practically empty. They asked how I'd spent my time. I merely smiled.

The End

© John Spencer 1991

Recycling

"It doesn't taste bad even though there isn't much of it," remarked the chesty Sandra as she adjusted her long blonde hair away from her plate and back over her alluring bosoms, which were trying to break out of her low-cut blouse. "He might not be at the pinnacle of society, but I always said Alf could cook," asserted Brian, the merchant banker. Judy, Alf's wife and the hostess of the gathering began collecting the empty dishes.

Two hours earlier, Brian had picked up Sandra from her flat in the Porsche. "Why do we have to go to a bus driver's boring little dinner party anyway? I'd much rather go to the casino and have a bit of fun," moaned Sandra.

"My sister Valorie roped me into it, and besides, it's good to keep in touch with ordinary people from time to time," responded Brian condescendingly, "It makes us appreciate how lucky we are."

"Would you like to see Alf's experimental vegetable garden before dinner?" Judy had offered when they arrived. "He's more than just a green thumb, you know; by using rotten fruit as a mulch and some clever grafting, Alf has produced some phenomenal potatoes."

"No thanks," Brian had replied before being interrupted by his voluptuous girlfriend, "I'm surprised Alf has time for gardening with all that exciting bus driving he does," she sneered,

At 7:30, Valerie had arrived, and dinner been served. Valerie was a voracious eater and never refused invitations involving food. She and Judy had been school chums some ten years before. In between mouthfuls, she chattered about anything and everything. "What adorable little hanging pots," she remarked.

"Whatever are they made of?"

"Those, those are made out of old egg cartons," answered Alf.

"What about the 'shell' lampshades?" she continued.

"Plastic milk containers and ice cream buckets."

"Some people just can't bear to throw out their old rubbish," sniggered Sandra, her cleavage catching Alf's gaze.

"Recycling' s in at the moment, darling," chimed in Brian. "It's so clever, and not everybody can afford to buy real things." Changing the subject, Judy spoke up. "It's so awful what's happening in Bosnia with all those suffering people, don't you think? Surely somebody should be able to stop it!"

"Why should we care if they want to kill each other?" scoffed Brian, "Leave them to it, that's what I say, And besides, wars are good for the global economy,"

"I should think Alf would be able to make something out of all that wreckage," quipped Sandra, crossing her succulent thighs as if to mock Alf further. "Just think of it, darling little doorbells built out of bomb fragments and nutritious garden fertilizer made from all those body parts lying around everywhere," Alf couldn't entirely hide a hostile glare; Judy turned to Brian. "Have you handed in your last year's phone books yet? It seems they can make wonderful kitty litter out of them. We put in ours last week."

Brian smiled. "Of course. I reckon one of those Sega mega drives they're giving away would look good on my coffee table."

"If only those silly French people would do something useful with that little atoll," interrupted Valerie, eager to get in her tuppence worth. "They could make it a solar-nuclear power plant rather than wrecking it with those stupid bombs."

"Yeah, and I don't want my Porsche to glow in the dark either," said Brian, "What could you do with Mururoa Alf?" he added just as Valerie was scoffing the last of the desert. This time, Alf didn't answer. Sandra wiggled her tits provocatively and took the opportunity to speak for him. "I bet he could turn the whole place into a gigantic underground garbage dump with a kiddies' carnival and fairground on top of it.

Excuse me, Alf, 11 Brian inquired." Er... don't suppose you have any more food? I'm still just a bit peckish,"

"Well, I'm still starving!" interjected Sandra, twisting her tempting body to show how slender she was. "I miss those feasts that the casino restaurant puts on."

"I do have some 'salad plus' food that I have been experimenting with," Alf proffered, "It's perfectly natural, but I shouldn't think it would appeal to you,"

"Never mind, if I don't get some more sustenance, I feel as if I'll die," crooned Sandra. Speaking for Brian and herself, she added, "Give it to us."

Alf disappeared to the kitchen for a few moments and returned with two plates of an unrecognizable kind of mush that reeked of garlic. Not being too strong on good manners, both the blonde and the merchant banker hoed into the alternative food. Between mouthfuls, Sandra commented, "It's got a rather earthy taste and an aroma I can't quite place, but it is food," Still munching, she then exclaimed with pride, "I can't believe that I'm doing something so new as test tasting a novel kind of natural food," "You're not doing anything new," retorted Alf. "Blowflies have been doing it for thousands of years."

"What's that?" asked Sandra. "Eating shit!"

The End

© John Spencer 1995

<u>The Beach, Sand, and More</u>

A young Chinese girl of 18 had winked at me as she passed by on the street. I had followed her, and the magic had begun. Three days later, after a couple of unsuccessful attempts at a rendezvous, the delicate little thing met me behind a movie theatre and invited herself to my hotel. Hot physical love, and she was mine. I possessed her mystical charm. Sindy was passionate and hot and was one helluva good root. Her slender physique boasted proud breasts, which were full and of a good size for a Chinese. Her hard flat stomach and sleek rounded thighs met at a steamy delta with a goodly thicket of pubic hair, and the shapely cheeks of her arse fitted the palms of my hands nicely. Her carnal desires were virtually insatiable.

A week later, Sindy and I attended a picnic on Battafaringi Beach in Penang. After an hour or two of swimming and social chatter, the urge struck her, forceful and unrelenting. She wanted it badly, and she wanted it now! Not surprisingly, perhaps, the Malaysian government, an august, largely Islamic body, held a fairly dim view of public copulation. Dutifully, I led her up the beach away from the others. Behind some rocks at the foot of a cliff, at the far end was a private patch of sand. Off went the bikini bra; off came the bikini panty. Her silky pussy and its triangle of forest lay there, begging. It didn't have to beg long, I can tell you. Forceful, fast, thrusting orgasmic love hit the spot, and the muscles of her tight vagina closed hard against my eager, pulsating cock. Two lengthy explosions had slaked her thirst for an hour or so.

The picnic finished in due course and we caught the bus back to Georgetown. As the high-structured vehicle rounded the bend on the cliff tops, I glanced out a left-hand window. There, down below, I spied our "private" patch of sand, in perfect view from the highway.

The End

© John Spencer 1994

The Mermaids

I have always loved the water, lagoons, rivers, and the deep blue sea. Water is the source of all life and all love. All dreams and all beauty trace back to the water. Bikini-clad girls or those bereft of such covers are always there to remind us of the beauty of Nature when we visit the beach. The sexual energy of the swirling waves challenges our male egos, and we are compelled to accept the dare of the elements. The excitement, the danger, the joie de vivre, the...?

We all know that lifesavers are definitely male, male, male, and therefore, there is absolutely no point in drowning if you are a bloke. However, man's bravado does not end with the bullfights in Spain. There I was at the beach with some girls. The breakers were almost Hawaii level, six meters high or more. It was late spring, and the water was none too warm either.

I had just finished telling the girls what a fantastic swimmer I was when this really spunky 16-year-old brunette spotted a shark. Sure enough, the fin of a solitary grey nurse could be seen about seventy meters offshore. "I bet you're too chicken to go swimming now!" she said, wiggling her sexy little body. I ask you, "What could a feller do?"

In I went, struggling hard against the breakers to reach the lonely shark. I was within ten meters or so of the beast when he decided to head for New Zealand, and I was left alone with the swirling waves. The beach seemed very far away, and I couldn't see the girls anymore. I think they must have gone home. The waves became bigger, and the shore seemed gone altogether. Water crashed into my mouth; I couldn't breathe. I was drowning! Never mind the effin' sharks! The last of the would-be mucho men prepared to meet Davy Jones.

At that precise moment, I could vaguely hear a whistle blow. "Thank Christ, the lifesavers must be on duty," my wet and salt-soaked being thought. "I hope I don't get a gay one. All that mouth-to-mouth resuscitation." It's strange what the mind thinks when you are drowning. Another huge wave hit me, and I was barely aware of my predicament anymore.

As I was going down for the last time, this beautiful, stunning girl grabbed hold of me and pushed me up. "I must be dreaming; death isn't so bad after all," I struggled to think. No! It was real. A gorgeous creature had hold of my entire body and was in the process of saving my life. She was wearing the briefest of bikinis, but boy, could she swim.

The waves were truly colossal, and by the time we reached the sand, her bikini, such as it was, had been washed away. She carried me up the beach and laid me down. My groggy eyes could hardly focus on her exquisite breasts and that tempting tuft of hair between her legs. I think it was the sight of her thighs and bum that revived me. But I could be wrong. The mouth-to-mouth was such that I felt like drowning again.

When I finally regained full and total consciousness, all I could say was, "But you're a girl!" Her reply caused me to totally pass out. "Haven't you heard of Women's Lib?"

The End

© **John Spencer 1994**

Powerful Pussy

I've always been obsessed with women in authority. Yes, it all began in primary school; those spunky, cool darlings that they called 'student teachers' and who, in their innocence, wanted

to mother us. And, if you were really lucky, your class could 'score' a sexually charged, regular teacher or school librarian. Yep, there's learnin' and learnin'.

While only some of us went as far as Thommo - who was exposed to the world as a wanker when the nubile young French teacher lifted his book to find out what he was hiding under it - we

all lusted and lusted. When I left high school, this preoccupation with sexy female authority figures deepened. With the introduction of young, pretty girl traffic police, the idea of being 'busted' took on a whole new meaning.

"We're going a little fast today," or "We're hot for action, are we?" would break the silence as a pair of firm, perfectly rounded, and succulent young breasts squirmed to break free of the prison of blue uniform. As the officer bent a little to write, occasionally, a glimpse of a potentially juicy upper thigh would challenge my eyes as the blue skirt fought in the breeze. Whether she was pleased to see me or not, the pistol was definitely not in her pocket, and its natural menace, glinting in the morning sun, somehow oozed sexual promise.

A two-week stint in jail (for non-payment of fines) didn't cure me either. I just got lucky. Every morning, as I stood there in my prison pajamas, the heavy, steel cell door would be thrown open, and there would be the shapely form of one of two lady warders. Some days, it was a blonde of about 25 who demanded I come forth. On others, it was a Polynesian princess whose love potential was far beyond the power of a grey screw's uniform to deny. When I was released and, a male warder with a gravelly voice chuckled, "Come back soon; I need the job," I could only think of those two goddesses of imprisonment.

Time spent off color was a joy in itself. The cold spoons of pulsating nubile nurses were no match for my lust for authority and power. Once, I really struck it rich, miserably, inching my way into an inner consulting room of a clap clinic, I was confronted with a chirpy and youthful blonde doctor. She even had an encouraging smile in addition to knockers and thighs from a modeling magazine. When she ordered me to show my 'tockley,' I couldn't comply quickly enough. She didn't laugh at it, but.... (another fantasy)... rejected my offer to share the clap.

Traveling in Asia only made matters worse. Security guards with curvaceous bodies and shoulder-length, sleek black hair abounded. Often their weapons were strapped only inches from their immaculate little twats, which were silhouetted by their tight pants.

The guns were defenders of the prize within. "Bugger the bank or the loot," I would muse.

I'm still not sure if what came next was a dream or real. The tropical heat and gallons of cheap piss can easily blur the lines between reality and fantasy. I was sitting on a sunlit beach, alone, minding my own business. A young girl of about 18 in a striped, pink cotton dress and carrying an AK 47 and an Uzi sub-machine gun approached me, wanting to know what I was doing there and what I was looking for. "Silly question!" Obviously, I was waiting for something to turn up.

Maybe I had strayed onto a beach in an unsafe area - there are lots of civil wars and guerilla armies around, after all - and this tempting lass with all the hardware thought I was a white, Neo-Nazi, fascist, CIA type spy. Or she could have thought that I was a spunk.

Anyway, I told her I was waiting for her to come into my life. It seemed to work. She stopped pointing the loaded machine gun at me and began to smile. Life in a guerilla army must be frustrating, especially if your comrades-in-arms are pimply, doctrinaire jerks who'd sooner waste a dozen innocent people than lend comfort to a lonely girl.

This gorgeous creature with proud breasts and an arse that appeared a lot more sincere than the revolution began slowly to undress, all the time holding on to her guns. Then when she's finally starkus, her velvety pussy staring at me below the guns, she

backs into the water smiling all the time. "I want your body (alive) now!" she says. I surrender in such haste that I lose all the buttons off my shirt as I rip my gear off. As I head towards her, she drops her gun into the sea. Now that she's sure I'm going to come across anyway. Then, it wasn't a dream.

Anyway, I hope

The End

© John Spencer 1994

Two Gun Terence

Long, long ago, in the land of sunburnt tits and choked up, checkout chicks lived and roamed Two Gun Terence. In the beginning, Two Gun was simply an ordinary old bushranger with a particularly nasty habit. Whenever he held up a bank or a coach, he used to flash his old fella, hence the name "Two Gun." While carefully aiming his double-barreled shotgun at his female victims' bustline, he'd point his exposed donger at the spot where he figured their cunts to be. This was so effective that the terrified ladies would recoil in horror and generally faint. In stubborn cases, Two Gun would start to masturbate, which invariably finished them off. Consequently, an accurate description of this obnoxious individual was well-nigh impossible, and the authorities were powerless. Two Gun was so hideous that even his male victims couldn't bear to look too closely.

Like a particularly loathsome blow fly, this twin touch terror buzz- ed over the length and breadth of Australia. One fine day, in the far north, he decided to hold up the pub at Tennant Creek. The Shot Gun poked itself through the swing doors and into the bar first; Two-Gun and his mangy doodle followed after. All the men were drunk and already on the floor. The barmaid with shaggy black hair and healthy, generous knockers was leaning over the bar. Before Two Gun could speak, a huge python slipped under the door, crossed the room, and went straight for the girl, who wasn't all that ugly. The snake, quick as lightning, slithered up, over and down the counter, and struck under the wench's dress. Straight through her underwear and into her snatch, the angular headshot, a horrible scream, and the barmaid was dead. As the python withdrew, licking blood and pubic hairs from its mouth, it turned and faced Two Gun. He could only stare; his jaw, Shot Gun, and hideous John Thomas all lowered in apparent defeat. The snake spoke. "I am the Rainbow Serpent. My people and I are sick and tired of the white trash round here. You are an enemy of these blots on the landscape. I will help you." Two Gun was transfixed to the floor. The snake continued. "From this time on, your ugly second gun will still offend human eyes but will be somewhat larger." At that, the creature slithered away with phenomenal speed.

The pernicious little bushranger went on his merry way and continued as usual since nothing happened. Both his guns remained the same. His next target was a Brisbane convent, which regularly received large cash donations and had become prosperous. As he bailed up the Mother Superior and several of her sisterly companions, he performed his usual modus operandi. After all, such a nasty habit was hard to break. Shot Gun leveled, he exposed himself to the good ladies. C.c.c.rack; his revolting penis expanded to ten feet long and shot right through the good Mother, killing her instantly. Blood, crucifix, and bits of habit stuck fast to the wall behind. The Rainbow Serpent had been no liar.

Church and State were now in an uproar. A slimy, repugnant thing had acquired the power of the devil, and there was no stopping it. Flushed with newfound confidence, Two Gun burst into the bank at Camden, his fly undone and the Shot Gun loosely cradled. A pimply young man in his twenties and a buxom young woman of similar age were busy counting banknotes. The young man looked up and smiled. "Hello, Mr. Bushranger. I like you. You're so, so... big. Any chance of a blow job?" Two Gun leveled his 12 gauge and blew the teller away. "I hate queers," he mumbled. The female bank clerk didn't faint. Nor did she put her hands in the air. She stripped out of her clothes and stood staring at the bushranger. She had long blonde hair, treat nogs, a fantastic arse, and a totally tempting blonde bush surrounding her juicy fanny. The thighs that kept the whole kit and kaboodle together were no disappointment either. Two Gun let go of his primary piece, and it clattered harmlessly to the floor. At that moment, the girl rushed him. The smiling, holdup man lost his clothes before he could even think. The blonde pinned him down and rode his backup weapon for all she was worth. Juices flowed in a steady stream. It was wonderful for the first hour. The bank had closed, and there was no hurry, but the woman didn't let up. Every position imaginable and she just kept going and coming. Two Gun felt pangs of fear and, snatching the shot gun from the floor, made a dash for it, with the perpetual nympho in hot pursuit. He lost her somewhere about an hour's running distance from Paramatta.

Two Gun headed towards Adelaide, but somewhere along the way, a strange creature sprang out from behind a tree. A few seconds later, seven naked and beautiful girls appeared next to the creature. "I am the Bunyip of Hay, and you'd better make my day. By the way, these are my seven tarts, er... I mean wives. What are you going to give me?" A worried Two Gun pointed the 12 gauge, but it jumped out of his hands and landed on a tree branch. He unzipped his trousers and produced the big gun. The Bunyip smiled, and the seven gorgeous and naked women laughed. The bushranger started to shit himself. At precisely that moment, an even more grotesque creature than the Bunyip turned up. "I'm Mrs Bunyip, Mr. Bunyip's queen." She crooned. "I'm very liberated, and I think you're cute. You and I are going to have a quickie!" Two Gun's monstrous dick shriveled up in fright and retreated to the safety of his trousers.

He was surely doomed. However, an object in the sky was zooming towards them at great speed. It was a Bronwyn Bishop lookalike on a broomstick, "Two Gun is mine, all mine!" the repulsive thing cried. From the end of her broomstick, oozed a fluid that looked like high-priced champagne. The gaseous, vacuous mixture covered the Bunyips and the seven naked girls, and they vanished. If Two Gun had been nervous before, he was really sweating now. "I don't deserve this!" he swore. "I'm only a bushranger, not a fuckin' politician." He retrieved his 12 gauge and fired both barrels. The witch with the unfortunate face was blown to smithereens.

After that terrible experience, the bushranger decided to take time off from work and visit his favorite whore house in Ballarat. "Frolicking Fur" was exactly the way he had last seen it: the red and black painted eves and the suggestively placed fern pot plants. Two Gun quickly selected three of the best stunners in the joint. A redhead with a slender figure and a crotch that could make grown men weep clasped his waist with fervor. A raven-haired beauty with sensual eyebrows and thighs, her dress couldn't hide, quickly joined her colleague. And there was no way that the bushranger was going to omit Hilda, a tall blonde girl with proud breasts and a backside that could ruin priests, let alone choir boys, from the chosen.

Up the stairs, the loving foursome climbed until they reached the executive boudoir, a room with a sunken bath, colossal bed, and perfumed walls, all reserved for only very important customers. The naked four soon indulged themselves in utter abandonment. 'Orgy' wasn't the word; Love holes, pubic forests, milky white hills and backside ravines. Nothing on the moving landscape was safe from the bushranger's second gun. The three tarts tasted so, so good, especially the blonde Hilda, who scored a little more attention than the other two.

Unfortunately for this ranger of bushes, both pubic and public, somebody had blabbed about his arrival. Well aware of what they were up against, a hundred heavily armed police had completely surrounded that palace of pleasure. The most junior of their number had been forced to place 200 kgs of dynamite under the stairs at the entrance. He shook so hard he could scarcely hold the match.

Forty seconds later, the entire brothel, a goodly number of whores, the three scrumptious tarts, and Two Gun himself were blown high, high into the air, almost never to be seen again. Almost because the Rainbow Serpent was very displeased. He hissed a spell that cast terror into the hearts of both blacks and whites alike and then went into hibernation.

The ghosts of the three tarts to this day ride the skies astride Two Gun's monstrous shaft. The four of them can sometimes be seen on the wind, their orgasmic cries resembling the screams of banshees. It is said that whenever they pass over a police station, somewhere in the world, a cop dies. Our friends in uniform, if they speak of this entity at all, refer to it as "Waltzing Fuck Hilda."

The End

Night of the Black Sun

We are all familiar with black holes, those strange invisible objects that, unseen, lie in wait for you if you just happen to be carelessly whizzing around through outer space. The innocent, unsuspecting celestial traveler is suddenly sucked into their vortex with catastrophic results. In the same deceitful and malicious way, socially malignant traps hang around, unnoticed, on our own beloved Earth. Smith was an ordinary sort of bloke who enjoyed the finer things of life and the odd bout of depravity when he could get it. He had gone on a holiday to the East with his football team. A thousand sets of shapely legs and a thousand pairs of proud melons had paraded past his steady gaze. The lights flashed, and the beat got louder. Then he saw the succulent Emily strutting the stage, her sleek and slender backside throbbing to the music. First, the upper portion of her bikini was discarded, revealing a lovely set of chocolate hills, and then her panties were carelessly tossed to the crowd. Harry barely noticed her curved, shoulder-length black hair. His focus was steadfastly set on the blackest triangle of Venus he had ever seen. That V of black velvet tormented his mind. He just had to possess it.

Harry was very ordinary, too ordinary. The only way to satisfy his obsession had been a proposal of marriage to the shapely Emily. A ticket out of a palm-laden hell hole was worth putting up with Harry for. It would only be for a while.

Back home, Harry just couldn't compete. The used car salesman who walked Emily home from her job in the factory, the macho types at the Angler's Club, and her own expatriate countrymen all left Harry for dead. Although pregnant with his child (probably his, at least), she soon left. The divorce court was a foregone conclusion. The judge smiled slightly as he announced his ruling. "Affirmative action is the order of the day, and accordingly, Mr. Smith, you will have to pay starting Thursday." And so it went: property settlement, maintenance, and more. Harry was a ruined man;

child gone, house gone, and job gone. The library where he worked had been deprived of funding, and Harry was laid off.

From that day forward, Harry's life progressed strictly according to the laws of gravity. He was unemployed, impoverished, and lonely. Mr. Smith was well qualified for most research-based computer jobs and applied for plenty. The Public Service was the first organization, amongst many, to turn him down with no reasons offered. To pass the time he had sought to join Rotary and also proposed joining the local Bowls club. Everything was a bummer.

"We don't think your personality would fit in here," they had said.

A stoical but nonetheless miserable Mr. Smith fared no better with the ladies. Shelley, a foxy little brunette in her early thirties, had struck up a conversation with Harry at a bus stop.

Her smile, tight cleavage, and sleek thighs enveloped in a black miniskirt had all oozed promise.

"You seem so interesting," she had cooed early on during their first date. A month and four outings later, it was a different story. Shelley had quickly grown distant. "You're not responsible, Harry, and everyone knows you're a loser. I don't see any future for us.'

Lisa and Brenda were similar stories. After that, Harry wasn't able to get any vaguely feminine form to even go out with him.

There he was with a permanent holiday and nothing and nobody to enjoy it with. "Still, Harry mused, "life at the bottom has an inherent optimism. Things couldn't get any worse!" Wrong! Harry had been looking forward to taking his only child, a boy of ten, on a short fishing and hunting trip. The early morning knock at the door had startled Harry from his sleep. The policemen had been very polite and slightly sympathetic as they took away his son.

"I'm sorry, Mr. Smith," a constable explained, "your ex-wife has taken out an apprehended domestic violence order against you. You are not allowed to contact her or your son, and we are compelled by law to impound any weapons you have."

The court hearing two days later merely ratified the order. "Mr. Smith," the magistrate intoned with gravity, "it is common knowledge in this community that you are a reprobate, and we are obliged to regard the potential danger that you pose with the utmost seriousness."

"But why? What have I done?" begged Harry.

"Mr. Smith," the magistrate continued with condescension, "this matter concerns your potential for violence, not specific offenses. You have failed to prove to the Court that you are incapable of committing any acts of violence or domestic terrorism and pose no possible danger to the former Mrs. Smith, her child, or the community at large. Furthermore, the boy's school reports show signs of severe emotional disturbance and a tendency for delinquency. The cause is only too obvious."

"That's unjust," piped Harry.

"The law cannot be unjust, Mr. Smith. That is a matter of definition," smiled the person on the bench. "These orders are permanent as of today."

Ms. Emily Flufftail, the former Mrs. Smith, had gone from having gold between her legs to having gold in the bank and considerable residential holdings. A succession of wealthy defactos and one brief marriage and the world was her oyster. It wasn't all that easy to turn a bearded clam into an oyster with pearls and jewels, but she had definitely managed it.

The corollary and its conclusion were as surprising as the body of the tale. Ms. Flufftail's naked body was found floating face-up in her own luxurious pool, her initial prize asset exposed in all its glory and providing a serious temptation to a family of crows. There had been some talk of foul play, but Harry, fortunately, had been out of town and was beyond suspicion. One of Emily's countrymen, the young- and good-looking Mr. Lopecock Figuroverher, was the chief subject of investigations.

The very next day, Harry had received an offer of a high-paying corporate job in the mail. As he waited at the bus stop on his way to the acceptance interview, a gorgeous blonde in a dark green Jag pulled up and offered him a lift.

"Hi, handsome. Are you going my way?"

As he eagerly climbed in, he exclaimed,"! Can't understand why my luck seems to have changed!"

The blonde gazed into his eyes and purred, "Perhaps you've just escaped from a black hole; they're quite dangerous, you know."

The End

© John Spencer 1995

Heaven's Hide: A Lovebottom Tale

Unas Lovebottom was a man of great dignity and pride, a plain man's version of HRH Prince Charles, if you like. Unas was also an adventurer's adventurer, sort of like our own Dick Smith, although somewhat more down to Earth. Earth-daring exploits with the ladies caused Warren Beatty's escapades to appear like the fumbles of a cautious choir boy in comparison. Unas had seen and done everything except catch AIDS. So much so, in fact, that this heroic individual was seriously contemplating early retirement at the age of twenty four.

When Mr. Lovebottom breezed into the city on the harbor during one of his numerous world jaunts (he had forgotten why he had come) and had overheard, in a pub on Broadway, remarks about a brothel that ranked amongst the Seven Wonders of the World, his ears had bristled like antennae. Thus, our hero was on the next plane out of Sydney, headed for the inner sanctum of Oz. Somewhere north of Kalgoorlie lay "Heaven's Hide," the penultimate of paid pussy.

A less than imposing, dust-covered structure of two stories, which resembled a 'two up' shed, opened to a barren little reception area attended by a curvaceous redhead in her thirties with outspoken, voluminous breasts. She gazed at Unas through bored eyelashes. "We have three levels of service here," the receptionist mumbled in a monotone, "Standard, Deluxe, and Superfine. Standard is fifty bucks."

Although hardly impecunious the adventurer preferred to travel light and could only just raise the minimum fifty. "Always start at the bottom; that's what I reckon. Give me the Standard." Unas was promptly led to a tiny, plain room on the ground floor, which boasted merely a bed and a table. On that table were a pineapple ring, a can of whipped cream, and a bowl of strawberries. Otherwise, the cubicle was empty. An unimpressed Mr. lovebottom lay on the bed and covered his impatient member with a mixture of fruit and cream.

"I've found you at last," a silky voice purred, and the door opened to reveal a stunning young blonde girl without a stitch of clothing. Her lithe and sensual body moved over to Unas, the ashen triangle of her womanhood tantalizing his now wide-open eyes. "I just love strawberries and cream, not to mention pineapple on a stick," the nubile goddess crooned. As those molt ruby lips closed around their quarry, fiery pangs of ecstasy exploded in the man who'd 'done everything.' "Life could still be worth living after all," Unas mused.

The following day, he felt compelled to return to the scene of the crime. The buxom redhead focused her motionless gaze on the expectant figure. "What'll be this time?" she snorted. "I'd like to try the top end of the range," whispered Mr. lovebottom. "A hundred and fifty smackeroos, Darling," smooched the face above the colossal mammary glands. Again, Unas was a little light on cash. After savaging his wallet and scraping coins, he could only produce a hundred. "Guess you'll just have to settle for the Deluxe," smirked Big Red.

Accordingly, Unas followed her up a flight of stairs to a rather opulent, rouge, and velvet-lined quarter on the left side of the building. The love den was deserted save for the odorous presence of a large, particularly bristly sow, which was happily chewing some rotting vegetables on the floor.

No words could possibly describe this adventurer's thoughts and feelings at such a moment. The idea of poking the insalubrious rear end of a porker didn't exactly inspire the heights of carnal desire. Nevertheless, Unas had always been a thrifty man and loathed waste. Closing his eyes and sneaking up on the unsuspecting creature from behind, he got his money's worth.

Although disenchanted, this raunchy raider was hooked. He just had to experience the Superfine treatment. After several days of indecision, he once more found himself in the dusty reception of Heaven's Hide. "I know what's on your mind today," smiled the redheaded gatekeeper with an upfront presence. "If you've brought a hundred and fifty, you're in." Again,

Unas was taken upstairs but, on this occasion, was shown to a generous-sized wood and saw- dust affair to the right. Inside was a goodly crowd of working-class men, shouting and jostling for position at the center of one of the walls. A minute or so later, a gold-miner type noticed Unas's presence. "There's a new guy!" he bellowed. "Let the new guy have a look." The mounds of heaving elbows and flesh parted, leaving visible a small spy hole. Pressing his left eye up against it, Mr. Lovebottom peered through. In the adjoining boudoir, a pair of absolutely gorgeous lesbians were ecstatically engaged in passionate and frantic lovemaking. Blonde on brunette, brunette on blonde; succulent tits, rounded bums, juicy fur-burgers; licking, sucking, inserting, teasing. A spectacle of frenzied, orgasmic excitement greeted Unas's eye.

"Holy shit!" cried the adventurer amidst tears of joy. "This is truly wonderful. I've never seen anything like it." A dour-faced giant of a man turned and laughed. "That's nothing, mate! You should have been here last week. There was a guy screwing a pig!"

The End

© John Spencer 1994

The Spy

It was the first day of my new job. Getting up at 4 am to enter the bowels of North Sydney Post Office by 6 was absolute hell. I've never been much of an early riser, and the prospect of flicking thousands of letters all day in the box room didn't exactly enthrall me either. Still, I did my best. At that hour of the morning, the buses were not too frequent, and the whole journey was a struggle. Stepping through the door, I glanced at the clock above me: three minutes past six.

"You're late!" a heavy male voice with a thick foreign accent boomed. "What's your name, boy?" I spun round to see a balding fat man dressed in the snazziest grey overcoat imaginable. "Albert Gardiner," I mumbled as the fat man scribbled in his notebook.

Proceeding to my appointed place, I introduced myself to a fellow worker. "That boss guy in the grey coat is pretty fierce," I observed. "Is he the Postmaster?"

"Hell no!" chuckled David, my fellow prisoner in the dungeon of paper. "Fredo. He's the cleaner. I wouldn't take any notice of him if I were you."

"What's he on about then, with my being three lousy minutes late and all?" David smiled the smile of one in the know.

"Fredo used to turn up here half an hour or more late every second day. He was told off countless times and nearly lost his job over it. Now the old bastard is forced to be punctual; he has decided to make damn sure that every else is."

An hour later, I had met all my workmates and was engaged in the earnest pursuit of repetitive strain injury, sorting thousands of envelopes. The grey coat appeared around the door, and the balding head above it scowled. "Can't you work any harder than that, you lot? You bludgers are all the same, getting your government pay at the public's expense. No wonder this er country is goin' to the dogs."

Twelve pairs of eyes spat hatred, with mine working a little harder than the rest. Stoically, we all kept working, ignoring this pestilence that went with our jobs. The grey coat disappeared, taking instant misery to another section of the establishment. "That man is such an obnoxious loser that even his own brother won't have anything to do with him," remarked Zelda, a hard-working Hungarian lady in her fifties.

The next day was similar. At a quarter past ten, Fredo's unwanted visage strode into the room. "What time did Alan go to morning tea? He should be back by now!" His question was directed to me.

"I was too busy working to notice, and I'm still busy," I sarcastically replied. I observed that the floor of our box room was desperately in need of a clean.

The following days were of much the same pattern, save that on the next Monday, I arrived at one minute past six. "You're late again!" screamed Fredo. I'd had enough, and my blood was beginning to boil. I was in no mood for this nonsense. "Fuck off, you overblown arsehole!" My communication was clear and to the point. At that instant, the megalomaniac came at me with the floor polishing machine, giving my shoes an unwanted shine. Grabbing him by the collar, I was going to job the bastard when the appearance of the Postmaster saved him.

Something had to be done. After conferring, the twelve of us in the box room decided that a cruel and vicious practical joke was in order. It was agreed. On a piece of official notepaper, the following letter was constructed and delivered to Fredo through regular channels.

"Dear Mr. Ambrosiac,

We at Australia Post Senior Executive Management are aware of the existence of serious staff problems at North Sydney. Laziness,

On the morning of the letter's delivery, the twelve of us kept straight faces and a watchful eye on Fredo's reactions. For the first hour he was hanging outside the Post Master's office until the Postmaster reprimanded him. "Mr. Ambrosiac, I don't think you have time to waste when the sorting room is waiting for a major cleaning." At 7:30, Fredo, his grey coat and notebook, snuck into the box room, the beady little eyes piercing through the gloom.

Zelda turned to me with a confidential grin. "It's the first time I've ever seen Fredo actually smiling." We all chuckled quietly, looking forward to the appointed day when Fredo would trek over to Surry Hills after work to look for the third floor of Surrey Hills Post Office. "The poor bastard got a shock when he found out that there isn't a third floor," sniggered David.

The following Friday, Fredo came to work with an angry, depressed look. "I dunno which one of you bastards has done this, but I'll get you!" he screamed. We all laughed and laughed until the Post Office resembled a lunatic asylum more than a government institution. An hour of work went by, and then the Postmaster called everybody together and congratulated Fredo on his promotion. Our jaws dropped. "Head Office," the Postmaster went on, "has promoted Mr. Ambrosiac to administrative grade three and appointed him as Box room supervisor."

The End

© John Spencer 1995

The Sandman

Ralph smiled at the stewardess and drank the last of his coffee. It was 4 am, and they were 40,000 feet above the northern coastline of Australia. He carefully opened the packet in front of him. Inside was $10,000 cash, a photograph of a stunning blonde, some printed notes, and a brief typewritten instruction, "Terminate." The photograph and the cash went into his pocket. The notes and instructions were flushed down the toilet.

For almost twenty months now, Ralph had worked as a sandman for the Keng Wong, one of the newer and more ruthless triads. Although born in Camberwell Green, South London, he had moved to the Crown colony as a teenager along with his family. During his six years as an undercover police officer Ralph had got to know the right people and the wrong people. His financial difficulties resulted from his greatest interest in life: women, beautiful, expensive women. Being moderately handsome with a dark complexion and aquiline features wasn't enough. He had to be a big fish in a big pond.

Now thirty, Ralph lived in the ultimate fast lane as one of the jet set's predators.

"Good morning, Sir. Welcome to Australia. Anything to declare?"

"Just a six-inch weapon in me trousers, Guv," Ralph joked with a churlish grin. The lined, weather-beaten face of the customs man scowled, and Ralph walked on.

After a twenty-minute cab ride, Ralph checked into a rather opulent sixth-floor room at the Regent. Three hours more sleep, and he was ready for work. There wasn't much slow about Ralph. Not much at all. He would complete his assignment in less than two days and then return directly to Hong Kong. He collected his equipment, a 9 mm. With a silencer, Walther went from a restaurant on Dixon Street and then caught a bus to Bronte.

Stella was a particularly fine specimen of Australian womanhood. In the last year of her teens, she was tanned and muscular, yet still feminine. She had initially been recruited as a courier while on holiday in Malaysia and now was the proud owner of a luxury apartment in the eastern suburbs and a white MGB sports car. Whether she had become greedy or not was impossible to say. But she had been seen on two occasions in the company of a Sydney drug squad operative. A week after the second one, Ralph had received the usual phone call and was on his way. The triad didn't like to take chances.

The third bar Ralph entered was the "Cock N' Bull", an English style pub, very popular with the trendies. There, propped against a bar stool, was his quarry, her long blonde hair running down over her white T-shirt and licking at her bustline. A rather drunk man in his twenties was unsuccessfully attempting to put his arm round her.

"C'mon, darlin'," I know you want it. It's perfectly natural and healthy."

Stella was desperately ignoring the stranger, but he was taking no notice. Ralph strode across the room and positioned himself between the couple, his back to the man.

"It's ages since I've seen you. You look marvelous." Ralph smiled straight into her eyes. The drunk glared and then shuffled away to try his luck with a pimply brunette across the room.

"That was sweet of you," the blonde whispered. "I'm Stella, Stella Mackenzie." Ralph introduced himself using his chosen alias. He liked this part of his work. He liked it a lot.

The girl gazed at him for a second and then, throwing her arms across his shoulders, kissed him hard. There wasn't any need for small talk. At the end of a short ride in the MGB, Ralph found himself in the living room of Stella's apartment, overlooking the dark, rolling breakers of Maroubra Beach. She produced a large joint, and the acrid blue smoke filtered up towards the ceiling. Ralph normally took no illicit drugs whatever, but his hostess was too charming to refuse. When they had finished the smoke, he was feeling slightly giddy and a little strange.

The girl led him to the bedroom and, still looking at him, pulled off her shirt. Her breasts were firm and full, and the pink nipples protruded defiantly. A small scar caused by a cigarette burn spoiled an otherwise perfect torso. The errand boy for Keng Wong was careful to remove and fold his shirt, which he placed by the bed, and the shoulder holster was carefully concealed. As he gently caressed her breasts round and round with his tongue, Ralph's left hand unbuckled her belt and opened the zipper on her jeans. They slid to the floor with a small "clunk." Stella's panties were plain and white but were of the rather brief variety. The small, rounded cheeks of her arse fitted perfectly in his cupped palms. The outline of her pubic mound stared at him with an urgent sexuality. Ralph could kill clearly and coldly, but he also knew how to fuck. "One thing at a time" was his motto, and he wanted the girl with the proud tits and the sleekly outlined snatch. Rubbing his hand on the insides of her thighs, he could feel her muscles perceptibly tighten. They fell together onto the expensive, blue sheets. Locked together in a powerful embrace, his manhood strained at its target.

Slowly and deliberately, Ralph stroked Stella's breasts and her flat, taut stomach. The heat from between her legs seemed to burn. Neatly and noiselessly, he slid her briefs down those shapely, tanned thighs and calves until they were free in his hand like a prize. Resuming his exploration, he discovered a thick, grey-blonde bush of pubic hair, which formed an almost perfect triangle. Stella's entrance was warm and moist. Ralph kissed and tenderly savored every part of that channel he could reach. Her soft moaning seemed to hang in the air like the summer sound of crickets. Having discarded the last of his clothing, Ralph gently climbed on top of the girl and pushed deep into her pussy. The slippery, steamy embrace seemed to last for hours. The grass had slowed everything down. His rocklike penis belonged in that passage, and energy drained from her to him and back again.

From time to time, Ralph's little finger wandered down to a very swollen little muscle at the top of her inner lips. Everything was pulsating. The room with its pastel curtains disappeared. There was only Ralph and Stella locked in an almighty coitus. The dope had slowed his body functions, but finally, he could hold on no longer. With a desperate, final thrust, he pumped a virtual river of jism into that throbbing cavity.

The girl fell asleep in his arms. There was no love in Ralph except a carnal love, and for the moment, that had been slaked. It was time for the Sandman to earn his wages. A fully dressed Ralph, with his dark wavy hair still soaked in sweat, gazed down softly at Stella's sleeping, naked form. He cocked the Walther, bent down, and kissed her on the cheek. Then, with all the precision and sentiment of a machine, he placed the barrel next to her temple and blew her brains out.

Barely twenty-four hours later, Ralph was back in Kowloon. He had never personally met Tan Lu Chin, the sixty-year-old founder and chairman of the Keng Wong triad, but he knew his phone voice well enough. Some months were quiet; others kept Ralph extremely busy. Now was one of the latter times. A certain policeman from Interpol was asking awkward questions around town. Not much to go on this time. The only lead was a bar in Tsim Tsat Tsui called the Opal Jade. The mamasan there, a hard-faced woman in her thirties, often knew things, and a girl by the name of Sandy, who had fled from mainland China, was used as a courier by the triad on an irregular basis.

Ralph took his place at a table and ordered a bourbon and soda. Despite its name, the Opal Jade was decorated almost entirely in red: red carpets, red curtains, and rich leather lounges of burgundy. Ralph called over the mamasan and made some discreet inquiries.

"I not know. You talk, Sandy. Maybe she know something." Jenny, the mamasan, scurried away. Before he'd had time to approach the girl, she came directly to Ralph's table and sat down.

"You very handsome man," she beamed. Ralph tried to suppress a self-satisfied smile but failed. Sandy was twenty-one years old, tall for a Chinese, and quite stunning. Her black, shiny hair curved round near-perfect features and stopped an inch above her shoulders.

"Have you seen any unusual foreigners around here?" he whispered. No answer. The girl was a businesswoman. No warmth lay behind that beauty. She wanted customers and money.

"You want nice blow job? I give very nice blow job. Make you smile for a week." Sandy placed a finely manicured hand on his thigh and, without a hint of a smile, kissed him on the mouth.

"It's a dirty job, but somebody has to do it," Ralph mused to himself.

The Sandman and the Chinese bar girl climbed the stairs and entered a small room lewdly and boorishly adorned with mirrors. Everything except the floor and bed was a mirror, and the heavy, thickly mattressed bed was in the form of a heart or, if not a heart, something of a similar shape. Sandy stripped off her silk dress without a word, revealing small, hard breasts and delicately contoured thighs. Her figure was slight but shapely and proud. Except for a pair of blue lace panties, she was naked. Still, without speaking, she pushed Ralph onto the bed and unzipped his trousers. Almost shyly, she flicked her tongue over his scrotum and shaft, teasing its head. Her lips parted, engulfing his member. Expertly, she glided her silk-like mouth up and down. Sandy's shapely lips seemed tireless. Ralph had always admired professionalism, and here was a girl who was more than good at her job. His sex organ ached with ecstasy, and even his balls were beginning to throb. The explosion that followed left him temporarily exhausted. As he lay there, he tried to question the girl but she was in no mood for talking.

Sandy began all over again, her buttocks straining within the lace panties. Her finely sculptured crotch was accented by the blue cotton. The dark nipples on her golden bosoms were hard and assertive. Suddenly, she stood up and, without looking at the man, pulled down that last vestige of clothing. The badge of her womanhood stared at Ralph, alluring. Sandy's pubic hair was soft and furry and very, very black. She glided onto Ralph's body, pushing his upright rod deep inside her. She was small and firm and very tight. As she drove up and down on Ralph, he grasped her backside and gently caressed the rim of her arsehole.

"Something about the Chinese," he thought. "Possibly the horniest chicks in the world. After all, it's no accident that there are millions of them." Sandy pounded Ralph until he was beginning to hurt. Her fine, black pussy hair was moist with sweat. The muscular lips of her tight little twat seemed to bite into the surface of Ralph's dick. When he finally came, it was like a sexual catharsis. It was as if this Chinese girl had sucked every fluid and every feeling out of his being.

She still didn't smile. "You happy now, right? O.K., pay me plenty." He dressed and handed over six hundred Hong Kong dollars. Ralph held another thousand in his hand and stared straight at her. "Do you know anything or not, Honey?" His words sounded dull and matter of fact.

"Nosey German man," she mumbled. "Last week, he here and asking many things. He not come back. Two days past, his body pulled out of harbor near Star Ferry. Maybe he fall in when drunk."

Sandy plucked the thousand from his grasp, tucked it into her blouse, and disappeared down the stairs.

After a relaxing week of drinking, gambling, and chasing skirts, Ralph found himself back on the job, this time in New York City. One of the triad's dealers, a black dude known as Johnny K., had been double-cutting their smack and trying a little private enterprise of his own. This dude was easy to find but a little harder to kill. He had his own goons on the street and inspired terror with all the ease of a banshee. Johnny dressed like a Calypso queen, but along with his jewelry, he wore a switchblade and a 32 auto. He was a mean hand with both. As well as several posh apartments in Manhattan he owned a sleazy short-time motel not far from Harlem. It was from here that he did most of his dealing. Johnny dealt in anything that would turn a dollar; coke, speed, you name it, but it was his connection with the triad that had made him wealthy. He had become big, and thought he was too big to touch. The Keng Wong didn't see it that way.

Ralph had collected his equipment and had begun his hunt. He had picked up some useful information in a dive called "Dalley's," and at around seven in the evening, he was passing an alley about a mile from Johnny's motel. The first shot slammed into a fence, narrowly missing his left ear. The second grazed his elbow, sending a burning pain through his arm. Ralph could barely see the two figures as he fired a volley from his auto. However, he was lucky. A bullet pierced the temple of one assailant, and another made a neat little tunnel in the neck of the second. Still clasping his bleeding arm, he checked the bodies. Both had police I.D.s marked "34th precinct." One read "Detective Inspector Bronowsky," and the other, "Detective Sergeant Green."

"Well, that's two pensions the taxpayers won't have to fork out for," Ralph inwardly chuckled. There was no time to lose now. Johnny K. must be on to him. Ralph dressed his wound back at his hotel. It was painful but not serious. A short taxi ride and he was at the door of Johnny's establishment.

"You want a room by the hour, Mac," the surly desk clerk grumbled, "Or can you manage a whole night?"

"I'm looking for Johnny," Ralph snapped. "The name's Green. Bronowsky sent me." He flashed the I.D., hoping that the clerk had never met Green.

"The boss's upstairs in the room on the left. But you'll have to wait. He's got a girl with him."

Ralph didn't have time to wait. He shot the clerk once through the forehead, dragged the body out of sight, and silently moved up the stairs.

"All right, baby, give it to me harder." Johnny's voice echoed throughout the room. Behind the door, on a dingy little bed, a full-breasted black girl was pumping away with the dealer for all she was worth. Her black, shiny body was soaked, and her legs were spread wide. The pink lining of her vagina was being pounded rhythmically and violently by Johnny's black snake. She was groaning, either with pleasure or with pain. On the floor beside the bed was an empty syringe.

Ralph burst through the door and fired a single shot between the dealer's eyes. The girl didn't seem to notice. She just lay there with his body on top of her. Ralph rolled him off. Then the girl passed out. "O.D.," the Sandman decided. "she'll be dead in an hour."

Ralph made his way to the subway. His latest assignment had been just a little close, a little uncomfortable. "Oh well," he reassured himself. "A miss is as good as a mile." He stood on the platform as the train raced down the tunnel. He didn't see the heavy-set, unshaven figure in an old overcoat. The tramp was standing directly behind him. The push on the back was sudden and hard. Ralph fell onto the tracks straight in front of the 9.20.

In the plush, extroverted office of Mr. Tan near Victoria Peak, the phone rang. Outside, preparations for the Chinese New Year were in progress.

"Tan here," he growled.

"It's done, Mr. Tan," the voice from New York crackled.

The head of the triad replaced the receiver and turned to his business partner.

"We always try to change our sandmen every couple of years or so. It keeps the organization tight."

The End

www.ingramcontent.com/pod-product-compliance
Lightning Source LLC
Chambersburg PA
CBHW061105100726
47911CB00012B/396